# Titles by

**Francis B. Nyamnjoh**
Stories from Abakwa
Mind Searching
The Disillusioned African
The Convert
Souls Forgotten
Married But Available

**Dibussi Tande**
No Turning Back. Poems of Freedom 1990-1993
Scribbles from the Den: Essays on Politics and Collective
Memory in Cameroon

**Kangsen Feka Wakai**
Fragmented Melodies

**Ntemfac Ofege**
Namondo. Child of the Water Spirits
Hot Water for the Famous Seven

**Emmanuel Fru Doh**
Not Yet Damascus
The Fire Within
Africa's Political Wastelands: The Bastardization of
Cameroon
Oriki'badan
Wading the Tide
Stereotyping Africa: Surprising Answers to Surprising
Questions

**Thomas Jing**
Tale of an African Woman

**Peter Wuteh Vakunta**
Grassfields Stories from Cameroon
Green Rape: Poetry for the Environment
Majunga Tok: Poems in Pidgin English
Cry, My Beloved Africa
No Love Lost
Straddling The Mungo: A Book of Poems in English &
French

**Ba'bila Mutia**
Coils of Mortal Flesh

**Kehbuma Langmia**
Titabet and the Takumbeng
An Evil Meal of Evil

**Victor Elame Musinga**
The Barn
The Tragedy of Mr. No Balance

**Ngessimo Mathe Mutaka**
Building Capacity: Using TEFL and African Languages as
Development-oriented Literacy Tools

**Milton Krieger**
Cameroon's Social Democratic Front: Its History and
Prospects as an Opposition Political Party, 1990-2011

**Sammy Oke Akombi**
The Raped Amulet
The Woman Who Ate Python
Beware the Drives: Book of Verse
The Wages of Corruption

**Susan Nkwentie Nde**
Precipice
Second Engagement

**Francis B. Nyamnjoh &
Richard Fonteh Akum**
The Cameroon GCE Crisis: A Test of Anglophone
Solidarity

**Joyce Ashuntantang & Dibussi Tande**
Their Champagne Party Will End! Poems in Honor of
Bate Besong

**Emmanuel Achu**
Disturbing the Peace

**Rosemary Ekosso**
The House of Falling Women
**Peterkins Manyong**
God the Politician

**George Ngwane**
The Power in the Writer: Collected Essays on Culture,
Democracy & Development in Africa

**John Percival**
The 1961 Cameroon Plebiscite: Choice or Betrayal

**Albert Azeyeh**
Réussite scolaire, faillite sociale : généalogie mentale de
la crise de l'Afrique noire francophone

**Aloysius Ajab Amin & Jean-Luc Dubois**
Croissance et développement au Cameroun :
d'une croissance équilibrée à un développement équitable

**Carlson Anyangwe**
Imperialistic Politics in Cameroun:
Resistance & the Inception of the Restoration of the
Statehood of Southern Cameroons
Betrayal of Too Trusting a People: The UN, the UK and
the Trust Territory of the Southen Cameroons

**Bill F. Ndi**
K'Cracy, Trees in the Storm and Other Poems
Map: Musings On Ars Poetica
Thomas Lurting: The Fighting Sailor Turn'd Peaceable /
Le marin combattant devenu paisible

**Kathryn Toure, Therese Mungah
Shalo Tchombe & Thierry Karsenti**
ICT and Changing Mindsets in Education

**Charles Alobwed'Epie**
The Day God Blinked
The Bad Samaritan

**G. D. Nyamndi**
Babi Yar Symphony
Whether losing, Whether winning
Tussles: Collected Plays
Dogs in the Sun

**Samuel Ebelle Kingue**
Si Dieu était tout un chacun de nous ?

**Ignasio Malizani Jimu**
Urban Appropriation and Transformation: bicycle, taxi
and handcart operators in Mzuzu, Malawi

**Justice Nyo' Wakai**
Under the Broken Scale of Justice: The Law and My
Times

**John Eyong Mengot**
A Pact of Ages

**Ignasio Malizani Jimu**
Urban Appropriation and Transformation: Bicycle Taxi
and Handcart Operators

**Joyce B. Ashuntantang**
Landscaping and Coloniality: The Dissemination of
Cameroon Anglophone Literature

**Jude Fokwang**
Mediating Legitimacy: Chieftaincy and Democratisation in
Two African Chiefdoms

**Michael A. Yanou**
Dispossession and Access to Land in South Africa: an
African Perspevctive

# Press Lake Varsity Girls

## Girls

## The Freshman Year

### Vivian Yenika-Agbaw

Langaa Research & Publishing CIG
Mankon, Bamenda

Publisher:
*Langaa* RPCIG
Langaa Research & Publishing Common Initiative Group
P.O. Box 902 Mankon
Bamenda
North West Region
Cameroon
Langaagrp@gmail.com
www.langaa-rpcig.net

Distributed outside N. America by African Books Collective
orders@africanbookscollective.com
www.africanbookscollective.com

Distributed in N. America by Michigan State University
Press
msupress@msu.edu
www.msupress.msu.edu

ISBN: 9956-615-49-8

DISCLAIMER

*The names, characters, places and incidents in this book are either the product of the author's imagination or are used fictitiously. Accordingly, any resemblance to actual persons, living or dead, events, or locales is entirely one of incredible coincidence.*

# Contents

Chapter One ................................................................ 1

Chapter Two ................................................................ 13

Chapter Three .............................................................. 19

Chapter Four ............................................................... 23

Chapter Five ............................................................... 33

Chapter Six ................................................................ 45

Chapter Seven .............................................................. 51

Chapter Eight .............................................................. 63

Chapter Nine ............................................................... 73

Chapter Ten ................................................................ 85

Chapter Eleven ............................................................. 95

## Other Books by this Author

*Honeymoon and Other Stories*

*Childhood Games From Lobe Oil Palm Estate*

*Real Mothers*

*Mango Fever*

*Sharing Space*

*Plantation Stories and rhymes from Cameroon*

*Imitation Whiteman*

To my mother, my sister, and my cousins.

# Chapter One

PRESS LAKE VARSITY: *The Only Secondary School in Kumba!* boasted the billboard to all who drove along that segment of the highway. And many did. These words, written in bold, white letters superimposed on a hunter-green backdrop, dared anyone to challenge the claim. No one ever did and no one would. Or will they someday? In any event, year after year, students flocked at the gates seeking permission to become part of the privileged few to be groomed at this "higher institution of learning" The boarding school promised its students more than education, as the principal reminded grateful parents, relatives, guardians and students each time an acceptance letter went out to that lucky prospective student. No one knew what that meant. In fact, what could possibly be *more* than education, some parents wondered. Anyway, prospective students all looked forward to attending this secondary school that stood proudly in a secluded section of Kumba town – K-Town as the local folks refer to this old commercial town in the South western region of Cameroon. How could they not look forward to going there? With a billboard conspicuously perched on a hill next to a highly trafficked highway, no traveller could miss it. The slogan on the billboard amused many, intrigued others and puzzled some even more. Granted, the tar on this part of the inter-city highway, made famous by Press Lake Varsity campus, had long worn off, overtaken by deep potholes, and thick slab of mud during the rainy season, while in the dry season the mud paste dried up and morphed into a dust storm choking pedestrians finding their way into the heart of K-Town. But then, it still did not obliterate the magnificent gated campus with a billboard that could be seen miles away. The dust piled onto the metal surface of the billboard coating the white carefully inscribed slogan that proudly announced this prestigious secondary school. Who wouldn't want to go to Press Lake Varsity? And of course, this was the pride of K-Town as one often heard parents boasting that their children went to the ONLY college in town. What that meant, strangers oftentimes did not understand. But they would nod and beam in support of the proud parent.

The students were also noted for their obnoxious or bourgeois attitude, depending on whom one talked to. They could be seen parading the streets of K-Town in little cliques ignoring peers from other schools especially those from neighbouring trade schools, just like their teachers snubbed colleagues who taught at such institutions. And worse yet, they would converse loudly in Standard English flaunting their superiority to the average pedestrians who spoke but Pidgin English. In their hunter-green and white uniforms, they seemed unrestrainable carrying themselves everywhere as though they owned K-Town – especially on Youth Day as they marched with wide grins on their faces along the tracks at the town square popularly known as Town Green.

As September rolled by one beautiful, hot afternoon, a new batch of freshmen also rolled into the campus for orientation. They came in brand new Mercedes Benz, in spotless Peugeots, in battered trucks, in dusty taxis, on old motorcycles with loads on their heads, but above all, they came in droves in chartered Toyota buses. It was a busy day for all at Press Lake Varsity and sometimes these Foxes – as the prefects checking them in often referred to the freshmen, forgot that they were there to receive more than an education. On arrival, the boys went one way and the girls the other searching for their different dormitories, which were located half a mile apart. Occasionally, a member of the opposite sex would stray into the wrong area only to be pointed in the right direction. When this happened the student would quickly look away, eyes darting from corner to corner in search of a familiar or friendly face. Only for the most part it was impossible to locate such a face in the overcrowded halls of strangers. This was the new life! It was a new life especially for five buoyant girls who had the misfortune of arriving later than the others on the first day of freshman orientation. What a way to begin life at this reputable boarding school.

First, Bridget arrived quarrelling with her mother over something. She was shouting at the top of her voice, dragging her overstuffed Key 16 suitcase with one hand and carrying an aluminium bucket loaded to the brim with koki and fried fish on the other, snack items to ease her way to the new school. As she stepped onto the concrete corridor that led to Dorm B, the dormitory set aside for freshman orientation that academic year, she brushed off some dirt from her shoes and waited for their houseboy to bring along her mattress and other bags full of her important stuff – she kept shouting for this shirtless hired hand to hurry or else. Her mother walked daintily into the room to check out the space her only daughter would be sharing with so many strange twelve and thirteen-year-old girls, some of whom she thought might be from interior villages. Urgh!!

"Tomas, over here. Place the mattress here. This Vono bed has stronger springs."

The houseboy carefully positioned the foam mattress on the twin bed his mistress had selected for her daughter.

"Now, make up the bed for her."

"Mama, I can do this like the others," Bridget protested.

"Shoosh! I am not asking you." Mama looked around searching for something. "Tomas, the sheets and pillow case."

Mother and houseboy arranged Bridget's snacks in one of the imposing wooden lockers that separated the spacious dormitory into two parts creating the illusion of having two distinct rooms for its occupants. She piled one item after another some in enamel bowls, others in plastic bags, stacking these items at the top half of the locker while leaving the bottom half for Bridget to figure out how she would arrange her clothes.

"Much better *na*, Bridget?"

"Yes, Mama."

Bridget headed for the door and bumped into another student who seemed as exasperated as she was.

"Watch it, you *bien nouris* girl!"

Bridget's mother gasped. Her daughter simply burst out laughing.

"All you do is laugh? You see why I wanted you go to Saker or Okoyong instead of this school that admits insensitive fools." Bridget's mother sighed and stormed out of the building leaving her chubby daughter behind to fend for herself.

Not long after all the parents had left, the drum sounded. At first, the girls did not know what that meant. Then Bridget suddenly realized. The excess flesh on her *well nourished* body flounced as she jerked forward.

"Run, run, you all," she chanted, brushing some students on her way out of the dorm. The others watched her in wonderment as she returned and quickly grabbed something before leaving again. They could not make out what it was that she needed to take along with her so badly. Her back disappeared somewhere in the corridor but they could still hear her panting and shouting:

"Run, Foxes, run for your lives."

Before they could grasp what she was saying, Bridget was already cruising toward a different section of the campus.

"Who was that *sef-eh*?" one of the onlookers ventured, as she continued to unpack her stuff slowly laying down one folded dress at a time on her freshly made bed.

"Who knows?" Another shrugged her shoulders. Then they heard a "kosh, kosh" sound on the concrete corridor right next to their temporal dorm. The footsteps approached: "kosh, kosh." Keys jingled. None of the remaining girls could speak for a couple of minutes. They just froze listening to the steps advance toward their room. Now they realized that they were the only ones there and that the others had already left. Only a handful of them remained in there packing and sorting out clothes and linens into little stacks, and snacks into little plastic bags. Most of their belongings were still scattered on their beds with some sprawling on the floor next to the metal twin beds. The footsteps stopped by the doorway and a shadow appeared announcing the presence of someone. As soon as the first girl spotted the dark shadow on the floor in their dorm she ran for the nearest window, mounted it and jumped over. Moments later, the others could hear her sprinting away outside. They rushed for the lockers and attempted to squeeze into the tiny space but only one succeeded. She slammed the locker door and hoped the others would go somewhere else. Instead, they stood by the lockers unsure of what else to do and waited for the owner of the shadow to appear. She coughed and leaned against the door, blocking their path. The girls waited hoping she would take pity on them. She poked her head further into the room and quietly counted them. After taking in the scene, she smiled, scratched her head, and coughed again.

"What do you people think you are doing?" Arms akimbo, she walked toward them, taking her time. The girls fidgeted. She could hear someone sobbing in one of the lockers.

"Come out right now, you Fox" she ordered.

5

The two girls in the locker dragged themselves out and joined the other culprits.

"You so, what is your name?" She shoved at the girl's head.

"Sarah, Sister."

"And you did not hear the drum?"

No response.

"Eh? Someone should answer me at once." Her voice squeaked. "This is not primary school anymore-eh. Do you all understand that?"

Sarah nodded.

"You know who I am?"

"No, Sister," she replied, lowering her head.

"You will soon know." The person's eyes wandered over the rest of Sarah's voluptuous body. She sighed.

"*You so*, you will bring us trouble. I can sense it already. Her eyes wandered again all over Sarah's already pubescent body. "Indeed, you will bring us trouble this year." She sighed.

"Now, you all run along to the Assembly Hall this instant."

"Yes, Sister," they chimed.

The Girls' Senior Prefect then smoothed her flare skirt and stared down at Sarah one more time. The thirteen-year-old freshman stood still, her heart pounding loud enough for Sister Dahlia to hear. The older girl grinned.

"Yes, you should be afraid of me. Be very afraid of me because I have my eyes on you." At that, she walked away, watching the freshmen scurrying off.

A few minutes later, they were all in the Assembly Hall, seated in rows – all eighty students that completed that year's freshman class - while the prefects and the administrators sat on the stage. As Sarah took a seat next to Bridget, she sighed and wiped off some tears lingering around the corners of her eyes.

"I think she hates me."

"Who?" Bridget asked.

"The Senior Prefect."

Bridget laughed. "I told you to run, didn't I?"

"So?"

"Serves you right." She giggled. At that moment, the Boys' Senior Prefect stood up and walked to the podium. All the murmuring stopped as the freshmen waited for instructions. They were not disappointed, for he asked everyone to stand up. Once all was calm again, he introduced the other prefects, explaining their different responsibilities. It was only after this that he handed over the podium to the Religious Prefect.

"Turn to hymn 704: 'Yield Not to Temptation'."

He tuned it so the students would have a sense of the melody and then he ordered everyone to sing.

"Now, sit down," he ordered in a monotonous voice. The students obeyed and waited for further instructions. The Boys' Senior Prefect returned to the podium.

"Form one students, the Principal of Press Lake Varsity."

The principal stood up and looked around the room. He paused for a moment, then grinned. With slow and deliberate steps he walked to the podium and watched the students again, most of whom he had interviewed during the admission process. He smiled and shuffled a few papers.

"How does it feel to be part of a great school like Press Lake Varsity, students?"

"Fine, sir!"

"What did you people say again?" the Boys' Senior Prefect interjected.

"Fine, sir."

The principal stared in the Senior Prefect's direction and waited.

He shook his head to the contrary. "Not just 'fine;' PERFECT. Let me hear you again?"

"Perfect!"

7

The principal smiled broadly and nodded in approval.

"That is more like it," the prefect added as he returned to his seat to listen to the principal make his usual speech.

"Students, today I welcome you to Press Lake Varsity, the ONLY secondary school in Kumba; the ONLY college where boys and girls are equal, the only place where gender does not matter. In Press Lake Varsity, everyone is a student and not a boy or a girl. You are STUDENTS and your parents have paid a lot of money for you to have the best secondary education money can buy in Meme division." He paused as students screamed excitedly. This pleased him so much. He watched them shouting and clapping for a few more minutes before clearing his throat.

"Alright, students, let the principal finish," the Senior Prefect calmed the crowd.

All was quiet again.

"Look at our beautiful campus; and we do very well in the GCE."

"Oh Yeah!" the students chimed again.

"Oh yes, that is why your papa and your mama sent you here and not to the others. To get an excellent education and much, much more. I can guarantee that!" He smirked. "So in conclusion, Press Lake Varsity is the ONLY place to be and we welcome you. And to you all who are females, Press Lake girls are NEVER shy. They are fighters like the boys. So we expect nothing less from you all. Welcome, form one students." With that, he stepped out of the Assembly Hall, followed by the Vice Principal and the teachers.

The Senior Prefect took over the podium, reading the week's agenda to the freshmen.

"First, as you all return to the dormitories" he began, "the prefects will check the items on the prospectus. If you are missing any item – and I mean ANY item on the list, you have no more than two days to make sure your parents purchase it. Do I make myself clear?"

8

"Yes."

"Secondly, you will all learn how to socialize with one another. And girls, you in particular should always remember that you are more special than your friends who bale out and go to those popular all-girls schools. You are now a Press Lake Varsity Girl! Nothing can faze you ever and I mean EVER!! So be ready to compete with your male classmates."

Bridget chuckled. She turned to a girl to her left.

"Look at the boys; are they really males? What would be so hard to beat in them? I am so ready."

The other girl shrugged.

Bridget carried on.

"What is your name?"

"Florence."

Bridget smiled wryly and looked across the room. In the row in front of where she and Florence sat was another girl. She seemed poised and unperturbed by all the excitement in the room. Bridget noticed what she was wearing and sighed.

"Florence, look at her; that one sitting over there calm like that. You think she will survive this jungle?"

The girl she was addressing simply laughed and looked away. Bridget sighed and turned to her right in search of Sarah the girl she had met earlier.

"What did you say your name was again?"

"Sarah."

"Sarah, look at that one over there in that delicate ready-made dress; do you think she will make it in this place?" Bridget motioned toward the front row.

Sarah burst into tears. "I do not know if I am cut out for this place. I should have gone to Okoyong or Lourdes."

"Come again?" The girl to Sarah's right invited herself into their conversation. "You truly do not know what you are talking about. Why go to a school where they cater mostly to rich people's children?"

"What do you mean?"

The new girl asked to switch chairs with Sarah so she could be between her and Bridget. Sarah agreed standing up to make way for the girl.

"Much better." Turning around she edged closer almost leaning into Bridget.

"Anyway, as I was saying, here, we have everyone; that is what my daddy who is also a PRINCIPAL said." She beamed and waited to see how they would react. "He said, go to Press Lake Varsity and you will see," she carried on stressing this last piece of information to her new classmates.

"Is that so?"

"You did not ask me my own name, why?" Without waiting for Bridget to respond, she rambled on. "Anyway, it is Magdalene; Magda for short. Schools with boys are good and by the look of it I can beat them like nothing!" All three of them burst into laughter.

"*Who be that one again?*" She asked pursing her lips in Florence's direction. Before Bridget could answer, Magda carried on, "she is all bones."

"Stop it now!"

"Okay, but that is the truth. You can give her some of your flesh and that would balance out very well." She chuckled and leaned into her seat, brushing against Sarah. "Oh, you on the other hand, you are perfect. Everything from your head to your toes! Life will be easy for you here, I bet." She laughed out loud again and focused her attention elsewhere. For the first time that day, Sarah smiled and raised her head up for all to see. She was perfect, Magda had said. Bridget noticed and slapped her hand. "Stop that!"

"What?"

"Just stop it. Boys will come after you and we do not want that, *na?* At least, not so early."

Sarah beamed even more looking much more older than her thirteen years.

"I give up. You will be trouble, I can already tell. Anyway, anyone knows who the *nyanga* girl over there is?

"She came today in a black Mercedes," Florence volunteered.

"What?" Bridget, Sarah and Magda responded.

"Uh-huh, a brand new one at that and not a *congele.*"

The girls paused for a moment to let the information sink in. At least, they knew someone on their campus who had actually arrived in a nice car and not the type that people got from Europe's junkyard – the congele that have taken over the streets of Cameroon! Bridget sighed.

"Her father must be rich then."

"That was what I thought at first; but I do not think so." Florence dismissed this, a little annoyed.

"Why not?"

"I just have a feeling. Anyway, look at her hair – long and smooth. I hope they ask her to cut it short like ours."

"Florence, *why you care so much?*" Bridget asked.

"I don't know; but I just care. See her, so delicate and yet . . . ; anyway, I give up."

"You people are funny," Magda added. "She told me earlier that her name was Annette – from Ekona, I think. Anyway, who cares?" At that moment, they heard feet shuffling around them and realized that it was time to go to their dorm. Like robots, all four new friends stood up and walked slowly in that direction, oblivious to what was happening around them until they bumped into Annette. Magda burst out laughing again.

"I bet your parents bought that dress from Printania."

Annette turned around to face the speaker. She smiled broadly. "How do you know?"

Magda grimaced. "Who doesn't know? See how delicate it looks and how hard you try not to rumple it. I gather, it is ready-made and must be expensive. There, you see, you are not the only one with taste on this campus anymore."

Annette sighed and looked away. And just like that, she became a member of this new group of girlfriends determined to make it at Press Lake Varsity.

# Chapter Two

The very next day, the five girlfriends and their classmates actually realized that orientation was serious. That morning when they woke up, before they went for breakfast, the Girls' Senior Prefect drilled them again on the day's activities: First make up your bed; next, do your chores, fetch a bucket of water, take a bath and go over for breakfast. It sounded simple when she had told them the night before. But getting up at 5:30 a.m. to begin the routine proved difficult for many, including Bridget and some of her new friends. And yes, they incurred their first punishment at Press Lake Varsity: one hour hard labour; they were warned.

At breakfast, the Dining Hall Prefect drilled them on how to use cutlery and how to conduct themselves. "Press Lake Varsity students must maintain proper eating manners," he announced before demonstrating how in a systematic manner, with each prefect leading at the eight different tables. At the end of breakfast, he reminded them of the importance of the first meal of the day. "Foxes." All the prefects burst into fits of laughter.

"Yes, you are 'foxes', if no one has already told you yet. And in our school, you eat well in order to perform well in class. My department will not fail you in that respect. Don't hold us responsible for slacking off in class, especially you girls! You must eat whether boys are watching you or not! You know why?"

He waited but no one responded. He laughed. "Perhaps you already know, but it is my duty to remind you in this refectory. You do not eat well, you will not do well in class.

If you feel the need to sacrifice your meals and academics because of a cute little boy who is eyeing you on the side, you are the loser. And of course, Press Lake Varsity girls are not like girls in other colleges who swoon when they see yam-head boys."

Bridget put down her cutlery on her plate and sat up. What the Prefect was saying made sense to her. She looked around their table and realized that Sarah and Annette had barely touched their breakfast. She gave them the evil eye and gesticulated that they should eat. Annette shrugged her shoulders and shoved her plate away from her face. She patted her lips and sat upright. Sarah's eyes reddened. She took a few bites and pushed the plate away when the male prefect at their table kept looking in her direction. Magda gave her a dirty look and she pulled the plate closer to take another bite. After breakfast, Bridget already with a piece of paper in her hand called a meeting to lay down the ground rules for their survival at Press Lake Varsity. She waved the piece of paper and they could see that she had already scribbled some of the rules on it. The four girls were amused but listened carefully as she read them one at a time. It went like this:

Rule number 1: No starving because of cute boys. The moment she presented this for discussion, Sarah jumped in. "And why not?" She sounded a little irritated.

"Look at you; you are not even ashamed to ask me that question."

Sarah bristled. "I do not have to listen to you anyway. Look at you." She ran her eyes up and down Bridget, wondering who had actually made her the leader. There was a tensed moment as nostrils flared.

"Enough of that, Sarah! Bridget is right. If we want to succeed, we need some concrete rules and that is not a bad one at all, especially for weak girls like you."

"Magda, you do not call me that, you hear?"

"I will call you whatever I want if you are to be my friend. If not, leave our group."

"Enough, you two." Turning to Sarah, Bridget asked, "Why do you not like that rule?"

"I just don't."

"Me, too," Annette added.

Exasperated, Bridget crossed it out and rephrased it.

Rule number one: do not starve yourself for a boy who will think he is your social and academic superior. "Does this version sound better?"

"I prefer the first version," Magda protested.

"Me, too," Florence added. Sarah and Annette said nothing.

"What do you people think?"

"I will do what I want to do," Annette said simply.

"Annette, we do not like your attitude," Magda added.

"You do not know me."

"Okay, Annette. Now let's move to Rule number 2," Bridget continued.

Rule Number 2: We will all strive to rank among the top 25 in the class.

Magda looked annoyed. Jumping up from her sitting position on the newly mowed lawn, she grabbed the sheet of paper and scratched out the rule. "This is nonsense! I am better than that. I will not fall below 15. You all know by now that I passed in list A with flying colours and could have gone to any school of my choice. I will not be beaten by more than a quarter of the class."

Florence giggled.

"I do not get your point. Are you saying you are smarter than the rest of us?"

"I think she is, Bridget. She just told us. Did you pass in list A?"

Bridget shifted uncomfortably on her seat. "That is not the point, Florence. We are making our survival rules and we need to make them realistic." Florence convulsed with laughter. "I think you are making rules that suit only you. I do not mind limiting it to 20 since there are 80 students in the two classes combined."

"Well . . ."

"Magda, I was on list A too," Annette reminded them. "Anyway, no one sets my academic goals for me. I know how I want to rank."

"You do?" All four barked at her.

"Yes," she said simply and looked at her wristwatch. "Go on with your rules. What is the next one now?"

"I thought you did not care?"

"I don't; but it does not hurt to know what you all have in mind. Next rule?"

Magda spat in disgust and restrained herself from lashing out at the show-off girl.

Rule number 3: Identify the subjects we are strong in and make sure we help girlfriends not strong in that area.

"That would be for you all. I am strong in all subjects. You name it - English Literature, History, Biology, Chemistry, etc. ALL! I am not weak in any."

"We hear you, Magda. But some of us may need help in some subjects."

"Bridget, are you sure about this? I do not think I am weak in any area. Well, maybe Maths."

"There you go, Annette. Sarah, Florence, what do you two think?"

"Sounds good to me."

"Me, too," Florence concurred.

"On to rule number 4; we are almost there. Five should be the max." Bridget went on.

Rule Number 4: Let no one be a CHEAP girl!

"What do you mean by that?" Sarah asked right away.

"Just what it means. We should live up to our full potential, and maintain that potential at all cost. This means not falling for cheap flattery."

"The rule does not make sense to me," Sarah insisted, pushing her throbbing bosom forward. They could sense her fury as she challenged the rules, chest rising and falling.

"Sarah, it simply means that you zip it up because we came here to study."

"Zip what up, Magda?"

"Eh-eh, you too; how can you pretend that you do not know what we are talking about, *na*?"

"Florence, let her be cheap if she wants to be. Now on to rule number 5, the last rule."

Sarah got up to leave but returned to her seat, fuming. Annette smiled, brushing something from her hair. "Look Sarah, if you do not like a rule, don't follow it. That is how I feel. No need to argue with anyone."

"I am not a hypocrite like some people."

Annette laughed. "You think I am a hypocrite? And how long have you known me again?"

No response.

"I didn't think so. *Oya*, rule number 5: Do not envy your fellow sisters!" She smiled. "How about that for a rule?"

"Not a bad idea at all, Annette." Bridget looked at the others. They all nodded, even Magda.

Rule Number 5: Envy of one another is not allowed!

They all burst out laughing. And Florence just turned around and said something none expected from her. "I think we have actually created a 'Girlfriends Club'!"

"Yes, indeed," they all agreed with Sarah, looking uncertain as they dispersed to do other things.

It was indeed a fruitful day, and even Annette could not deny this fact. Although she had no idea how it would work, or if she cared very much for the other 4 girls in the club. Magda, felt elated. It would be a wonderful experience after all, she reminded herself in her corner of the room where she continued to unpack her belongings. Bridget, Florence and Sarah simply disappeared to no one knew where; perhaps to prepare for the upcoming freshman socials that was typical at Press Lake Varsity. They had all been informed to be prepared.

# Chapter Three

That year the socials began promptly after dinner. As the Socials Prefect reminded the freshmen, it was an opportunity to prepare them for the social life at Press Lake Varsity. And so they needed to be prepared well before the rest of the school arrived. Annette and Sarah, as was to be expected, came in style, with their ready-made dresses outshining dresses worn by the thirty-something other girls who attended the occasion. Bridget and Florence arrived later, dressed casually. As soon as they entered the Assembly Hall that had been converted into a makeshift night club, Florence gasped. She nudged Bridget.

"Back off!"

"I told you we should have dressed properly for the party."

"We are dressed okay. Follow me," her friend replied curtly. They wangled their way to a section of the room where most of the girls sat. With plastic cups of sweet drinks in their hands, the girls looked frightened. They were wondering whether the Socials Prefect would approve of their party behaviour. Bridget and Florence looked around and finally spotted Magda at the other end of the room. She sat next to two skinny boys who kept stealing glances at her and smirking. Magda looked irritated and shifted uneasily on her seat. There were other girls in that area all looking sheepish as they sipped their drinks in silence. And as for the boys, some leaned back on their chairs not sure as to what was expected of them. Bridget took in all these and decided it was time to find a place to sit down. One more glance at Magda's direction she noticed her adjusting her dress pulling the seams to cover any exposed body parts. There was no doubt that she looked stunning in her maxi dress. Bridget waved at Magda in vain. Bridget sighed and decided to leave her alone for that moment.

"Let's look for a spot to settle in before contacting the others."

Florence agreed and followed Bridget. By the time they were seated, music was already playing and the Socials Prefect and the other prefects were already on the dance floor, demonstrating how the freshmen were to do it. Once seated comfortably, Bridget beckoned to the others to join them, so they could be together as a group. Annette barely cast a glance in her direction and mingled further with some guys who were standing aimlessly on the dance floor. Sarah hesitated, then walked over.

"What are you doing?" She asked right away.

"Girlfriends sit together at parties, don't they?" Florence explained, chewing something furiously to calm her nerves.

"So you tell me." Sarah looked across the room and saw Magda.

"Excuse me. I will be right back." At that, she left to mingle even more.

Moments later the Socials Prefect asked everyone to take a seat. Then the occasion officially began with him laying out the rules: boys must dance with girls; girls must dance with boys. The room was immediately filled with moans.

"Yes, you will learn to dance with each other: boy and girl, no exceptions. And no bone to bone or flesh to flesh."

He turned around to look for the DJ. "Play something so we can get this party going."

Instantly, music filled the air. He grinned and rubbed his palms vigorously.

"Now students, listen carefully; for failure to do as I say will lead to one hour's hard manual labour."

The music played on.

"Girls' choice," he announced finally. The girls, huddled in one corner cringed even more, trying to hide behind each other's back.

"I said, 'Girls' choice."

Feet dragged on the floor as the girls hesitated. But before Bridget could figure out what to do, Annette was already on the dance floor with a guy. The crowd applauded.

"Yes. That is how it is done. Press Lake Girls are never shy. So do your thing. Who else has the Press Lake spirit among you girls sitting in that corner?" The Socials Prefect looked from one angle of the room to another.

"You over there; yes, you," he beckoned to someone in a far corner. "Why hesitate when you know you really want to dance? Just pick a fellow and join the pair on the floor."

Magda, grabbed one boy's hand and they stepped onto the dancing floor.

"That's right. Press Lake girls are never shy, or else you would not be here. Isn't that right?"

Without waiting for a response, he walked over to Bridget's section of the room and beckoned for them to get up. Florence hid behind her friend and Sarah giggled.

"Hey beautiful, you can do it. Who will not want to dance with you in this room? Try me?"

Sarah could no longer contain herself. She walked over and asked a guy. By the time the music was halfway finished the floor was swarming with couples. Then the music came to an abrupt end.

"Applause everyone! Yes, that is how we do it. Now, boys, it is your choice next. DJ, do your thing. A slow tune filled the air.

"Boys, let's see if the girls are more courageous than you."

The boys remained seated. Some attempted to run out of the room but were accosted and forced back into the hall.

21

"Yes, let's see how you lead the girls in a slow dance. But remember, no cheek to cheek or knee to knee. There must be enough space between you two!" He chuckled enjoying every minute of the experience.

"I said 'boys' choice. Did you all not hear me, boys?"

No one was bold enough to do it.

"Shame on you, Press Lake boys. DJ another number; let's give them another chance to make up for the poor show," the Socials Prefect suggested.

Another tune came on. He stood silent for a moment and watched the students. They did not budge. "Okay, boys, this is how you do it." He went across the room and asked Sarah for a dance. She was so delighted she clutched his hand until they reached the centre of the dance floor. As they began dancing, one by one, the other males in the room joined them on the floor with their partners. The evening went like that until nine p.m. when the drum sounded for the freshmen to go to their dorms. Bridget heaved in a great sigh of relief. And so ended another day of orientation.

She knew it was just a few more days before the entire student body joined them. What would it be like, she kept asking herself. It was hard for her to imagine and no one talked about it as much as she would liked. Did the others not care at all, she wondered.

The days flew by with one orientation activity after another, and soon it was Saturday, time for them to pack out of their orientation dorms and head to their assigned dorms. As they stood out on the lawn in front of the Assembly Hall, in rows of four, Bridget fidgeted with her small handbag and waited for her dorm assignment. The Boys Senior Prefect read out the names slowly, and by the time he was done, members of the newly formed girlfriends club were separated into three dorms. Bridget took a deep breath and thanked her stars that she was in the same dorm with Magda.

# Chapter Four

Orientation week was just ending when the freshmen began noticing something. It was strange, exciting but worrisome. The crowd of older students as they streamed in with their luggage in buses, vans, cars; on trucks, motorcycles, bicycles seemed ready. But ready for what? This was a serious cause of concern for Bridget and the others. The freshmen leaned on the low walls surrounding their different dorms watching the senior – forms two through five – students arrive in style or what they thought was style. They came and the campus exploded with activity. In just one day! But as the weekend dragged to a final grind on Sunday, the freshmen simply vanished. They no longer existed, or so many of them felt as the older students brushed past them, talked over their heads or shooed them away from their path.

Bridget felt it. The others felt it but there was nothing they could do to stop the inevitable. This was Press Lake Varsity, the secondary school of their dreams. As the weekend wore off, Bridget searched frantically for her friends. She could see them nowhere. For the first time in her short life, she felt extremely isolated. Feeling abandoned and ignored, she convulsed into tears and roamed from building to building, dorm to dorm, looking for her girlfriends. How would she survive this mad rush all by herself? How was she going to cope among this wide pool of strangers? She sobbed some more and sat down waiting at the edge of the corridor for a miracle to happen. And it did, or so she thought until she saw who it was standing right in front of her. The older student tapped her on the shoulder and Bridget raised her head from her lap and stared at the stranger.

"Are you sick?" The older student inquired.

Bridget quickly dried her tears. "No."

"Good." The older student dropped her suitcase on the floor. "Now get up and carry it to Dorm B."

Without a word, Bridget obeyed. As she stooped to place the heavy suitcase on her head, the older student flung her carry-on bag on one shoulder and waited.

"Be careful with that box, you hear me, Fox?"

"Okay," Bridget managed a response. She balanced the suitcase and stretched her neck to accommodate the weight.

"Okay, what?"

Bridget was dumbfounded by this. She stood a moment and turned around to carry out the order, but the older student dragged her by the blouse.

"Okay, what, Fox?"

She sounded upset. Bridget's eyes reddened. She hesitated for a moment not knowing what else to say; then she remembered the college girls' etiquette.

"Okay, Sister."

"That's more like it." The older student grinned impressed that Bridget was already familiar with the respect of Senior protocol at Press Lake. "Go, go, go!"

Bridget lurched forward ignoring the weight of the suitcase. She dodged piles of luggage that sprawled everywhere on the corridor; brushed past girls arguing and so on until she finally arrived. Slowly, she placed the suitcase on a bed.

"Not there; over here."

She placed it back on her head and took it to the right corner.

"Now gently. Don't scratch my valise."

"Okay, Sister," she responded making sure nothing scratched the suitcase.

When she left the room, there was pandemonium everywhere with her becoming an integral part of the ruckus. There was not an inch of space to place one's foot on the

24

concrete corridor. Instead, there were makeshift pathways to accommodate the heavy student traffic and the tons of luggage that came with these people. Bridget was amazed. She turned to the right and turned to the left, but still did not know which way to go. She could see other freshmen hauling luggage back and forth with tears streaming down their cheeks. No time to ask questions, just grab and take to the right dorm or else! Or else what? Bridget did not want to think about the consequences, for she could not even begin to fathom them. As she tried to sneak out of the corridor, someone tapped her on the shoulder and pointed to several pieces of luggage lying on the floor not too far from where she stood. Not again.

"Yes, Sister."

A smile.

"I already like you. *Oya*. Dorm C."

"Yes, Sister."

Never in her life had she anticipated this or seen so many girls in one building at the same time. It frightened her, especially seeing how they kept shoving people's heads and ordering them around. Raising her head a little to grasp the full picture of what was happening, she spotted Magda across the yard in Dorm A, hauling stuff as well. Her face looked sour with displeasure; it was hard not to laugh. Bridget controlled herself, though. She looked again and this time their eyes locked, but Magda quickly looked away. Bridget chuckled.

"Fox?"

"Nothing, Sister."

"Hurry then. No distraction."

"Okay, Sister."

She worked harder than before increasing her speed. And before she knew it, she had already transported five suitcases, three sacks of garri and a bucket of something. *Weh*! She was on her way to haul some more when she noticed some movement in the neighbouring bushes. Her eyes lit up. Good idea. She looked around and everyone seemed pre-occupied with something. Her moment. She sneaked into the bathroom, leaving the senior student stranded. She could hear her calling out for the "fox" that was just there to assist her. Bridget did not budge. She waited there awhile. She was lucky that the bathrooms were clean that weekend or else . . . She did not even want to think about it. When she could no longer hear that Sister's voice, she came out of the bathroom and walked along the short stretch of the corridor with a certain degree of confidence. A senior student spotted her and was about to make her carry stuff. Bridget shook her head.

"Not me; I am looking for a Fox to carry my cargo too," she said, feeling important.

The senior student nodded understandingly.

"If you see a spare one, send her this way."

Bridget covered her mouth to suppress giggles and hurried down the corridor seeking out the nearest exit. Once she spotted one, she scurried away and disappeared behind the bushes.

"What a relief!" She exhaled as she took cover. "Annette, great idea, by the way."

"Ssshe!" her friend placed a finger on her lips and made more room for her.

"What gave you this idea?"

"Ssshe!"

They huddled there until the moving-in activities gradually died down.

"Now we can talk." Annette got up, dusting the debris from her floral print dress. She smoothed down a wrinkle here and there. They were just about to step back into the corridor when they heard Florence protesting somewhere.

"Sister, it is not fair!" she said loud enough for all in the surrounding area to hear. Bridget gasped. "She got it coming," Annette said simply and waited.

"Fox! How dare you?"

Annette laughed. "Here it comes."

"For that you will wash my plate for the next one week, you hear me, Fox?'

"Yes, Sister," Florence answered her voice heavy with resignation.

"I have to write your name. Name?"

"Florence."

Bridget chuckled as Fox and Senior disappeared somewhere. Annette had one foot on the corridor when Bridget turned around. "Did you see Sarah?"

Annette ignored her and waited in silence a while longer. Voices were finally dying down.

"We can go now. Sarah found a Big."

"She did?"

Uh-huh. Sister Dahlia. You know, Senior Prefect and all."

"Good God!"

"I thought so too."

"Lucky her!"

"Lucky Big, I would say."

"Now, you've lost me, Annette."

"Look at Sarah."

"Yes?"

"Look at her father. Or rather, look where her 'daddy' is?"

"What does it have to do with anything?"

"You'll get it soon enough," Annette said simply.

The two girls strolled along the corridor, which was now vacated. The place that had looked like chaos moments ago seemed almost bare. They could hear voices in the dorms, though. As they walked on, a door opened and someone called out if there were any "foxes" around. They ignored the speaker and walked right past the door, straight on toward another part of the campus. They could see the boys rushing back and forth down in their section of the campus – their numerous dorms that by far outnumbered the girls' dorms. Bridget smiled.

"So they too are hauling stuff!"

"But of course. They are Foxes too!"

Then a thought crossed Bridget's mind. "Do they have Bigs too?"

"Not sure; anyway, boys don't need as much taking care of as girls."

A certain uneasiness loomed in the air as they walked on in silence, just the two of them, without the others.

"I've finally decided. I need a Big too."

"You think?"

"Yes, Annette. I need one too."

Annette shrugged and gazed into the distance, observing the clouds shift in the sky. Then, just as she had shrugged it off, she took her eyes away from the clouds and looked right ahead of her.

"Bri. May I call you that?"

Bridget was startled. No one had called her that for a while, especially since her parents and siblings knew that she did not like the fact that they had named her after the wrong aunty. Worse, the aunty went by the shortened version of the name.

"Sure. Call me Bri," she accepted graciously then changed her mind. "I prefer Fese, though."

Annette made faces. "What?"

"Is there anything wrong with Fese?" Bridget barked at her.

"No, no, no! Okay, Fese – that will be my special name for you then. Anyway, having a Big is not an option."

"Suit yourself, although I still do not follow you." Bridget paused on her path and waited for Annette to make her point.

"It is an unspoken rule at Press Lake Varsity!"

"Is that all? I already knew that. Remember, my father is a contractor to this school."

"Really?" Annette's eyes lit up. "Is that why you chose Press Lake Varsity?"

"Don't get me started." She rolled her eyes.

"Okay. No need to explain." Annette dropped the subject.

Just then they spotted Florence. She saw them too and burst into tears.

*"This wuna school too much for me,"* she wailed.

"It is okay, Florence," Bridget consoled.

Florence had had it. "You know how many suitcases, trunks, and bags I carried today? See my middle head, I am almost certain I am already going bald," she sobbed.

"But it is over, *na*? Isn't that true, Annette?"

Annette shrugged her shoulders and before she could say something Florence carried on.

"No, no, no! Not for me anymore. I leave for home first thing in the morning. The ONLY secondary school in Kumba, my foot!" Tears were really pouring hard now; even Annette could no longer ignore her new friend's pain. She looked away momentarily to forget the pain she saw in Florence's eyes. She hoped to God that her eyes did not betray her own fears. Florence looked pitiful.

"This school is not for me-oh! What should I do-eh, Bridget? Annette?" She looked pathetic, crying her heart out like a baby. Her friends could not understand her irrational behaviour.

"Stay like we all are trying to; not so Annette?"

"Yes. Like we all are trying to," she said absentmindedly. "Where is Magda? Where is Sarah?"

Annette attempted to leave, but Bridget held tight to her skirt. "You are going nowhere," she gritted her teeth.

They waited by the sidewalk for Florence to finish crying. She sobbed on.

*"Dish washer na my first job for college. Weh!* Why do I have so much bad luck like this? Sister says to wash her plate for one week."

"So wash it!" Bridget was becoming impatient with how needy Florence sounded. What else could she do? Then Annette saved her the trouble.

"Go back home, Florence; or go to your all-girls school and see."

"What?" Florence was stunned at this sudden outburst.

"Yes, you heard me. Go and deal with an entire school of girls – SENIORS and all and send us postcards on how life goes on over there."

Bridget was dumbfounded. Annette brushed something off her dress. "Fese, ready for dinner?"

"I guess so." Bridget smiled, taking Annette's hand, and they began to leave.

Florence's eyes brightened. "You are so right, Annette," she shouted after them.

"So true. Wait up," she called after them. "I will simply find myself a good BIG."

They both laughed.

"Not a bad idea at all. Not so, Annette?"

"Me too, Florence"

They were almost at Bridget's dorm when Florence frowned.

"What now?" Bridget asked.

"One has already chosen me to be her Small," she announced. Bridget and Annette exchanged glances and concluded only Magda could handle the situation at that point.

During dinner that evening, Bridget dropped Magda a hint about it. She said she would take care of the problem – to give her time to think some more; nothing to lose any sleep over. After dinner, she suggested they all assemble in a classroom far, far away from the dormitories. When they arrived, Magda was ready with a solution. Her idea was quite simple: Florence should graciously accept to be this Sister's Small but then she should complain of headache or stomach ache every other week.

"How will that help her?" Bridget asked.

"Simple! Sister will eventually get tired of having an invalid for a Small and may decide to depend on free agents or freshmen who have Form four Bigs."

That sounded brilliant to the girlfriends. Bridget could not help but hug Magda. Everything always seemed so simple to this girl; she could not understand how that was possible.

They then turned their attention to Sarah. But she did not want to talk about it.

"I like my Big and that is final."

"Who said you did not like Sister Dahlia?" Florence laughed.

"You mock me? You with a devil for a Big, dare to mock me?" She grabbed her handbag to leave but Annette dragged her back.

"Not like that, Sarah. I do not mock you. We just noticed that she had one of your dresses on for dinner."

"Not true," Sarah protested, tears swelling in her eyes with each breath of protest.

They watched her foam and splash.

"You are all jealous of me. I got the Senior Prefect. She likes me. I do not believe that my own friends would be the first ones to be jealous of my good fortune. Rule #5 already broken"

"Believe what you want," Magda chimed in. "But she got you is all we are saying."

They all burst out laughing.

"Not funny. She made my bed up today."

Their eyes lit up.

"Yes, she did. How about that," Sarah rubbed it in.

"Lucky you then," Bridget said. "Anyway, enough about Sarah and Florence. I have found a Big too; sort of."

Annette raised her eyes. "Really?"

"Uh-huh; sort of. I still have to ask her."

"Good for you then. Me too," Magda added. All eyes turned toward Annette.

"I'll tell you all when that happens."

They exchanged glances and burst out laughing again.

"Will anyone want you at all?" Magda asked bluntly.

"I really do not care; when I choose one, I'll let you all know and that's that!"

"Okay, Madam."

The night was still young as the five girlfriends sat there contemplating their fate at Press Lake Varsity. It was a long, long night ahead of them but they were also ready for the promises it held for them and the booby traps that lay hidden somewhere. As it got darker, it got easier and even more hopeful, for these five girls, like the majority of students that frequented this institution, were always looking forward to sunrise. It would always be a pleasure for them to see the early sun rising from behind the dark clouds and toiling its way among the clouds to brighten someone's day. Especially days like the ones they had recently experienced as they made room in their lives for older students and new strangers. And, as Bridget reminded all five of them that night, there was nothing they could not face as long as they confronted it together. Nothing! They had all laughed this thought away as they nursed their secret fears and dealt with their inadequacies, which they hoped would take long to manifest themselves to the public. That inner fear of being the last one in the class; the wayward one in the group; the one from the poorest home; the one most found the least attractive, and above all, the one no one gave a damn about. As Bridget snuggled under her covers that night thinking about all that lay ahead for the next 5 years, she prayed to God that she should not fail her parents; and above all, that she should not fail herself. She could do it and would do it regardless of the obstacles that were placed in her way. She sighed and dozed off drifting momentarily into a world over which she had no control.

# Chapter Five

The day finally broke and the freshmen had the opportunity to finally attend their first college lecture. It was unlike any other day they had experienced since they left home and joined this new world that promised a lot and challenged them a lot as well. This first day that many looked forward to, filled others with trepidation – including Bridget. The first day of class. Hmmm! She was particularly excited though and felt like nothing could go wrong. And why should anything go wrong when she was so prepared to study, study, study; more so than she was prepared for the social life. And yet, she was already surviving that – with her friends.

It was indeed a promising morning that brought the sun out earlier than usual with its ray hitting hard on the black metal roofs that graced every single building on campus. It was splendid; Bridget thought to watch the sun glistening on overnight moisture with reflections that could blind someone's eyes – almost, but not quite. There was something serene about the campus now that school was in session with all the students heading to their different classrooms. She wondered why they were all there. Was it for the same reason – to become "somebodies?" Or was it just one more thing to do as they got older. She brushed the thought away and walked side by side her friends as they all headed to the Assembly Hall. The bright sun shone on everything below touching the heads of all the students that lined out there in waiting. It was a field of hunter green as uniformed students flooded the lawn designated for this purpose: morning inspection.

Teacher in charge: "Nails?"

Student performed act stretching out the fingers for examination.

Clean

"Teeth?"

Act.

"Hair?"

Act.

"Clean, clean, clean; step aside. Poor hygiene. Note that down Prefect; two hours hard manual labour."

The line seemed endless; but because the inspection seemed so methodical it went fast. By the time the teachers-in-charge were done, they had identified at least twenty students with poor hygiene. The girlfriends were not part of this unclean folks! Thank goodness, Bridget took a deep breath. They were then asked to file into the hall according to their class standing: Forms 1, 2, 3, 4, 5 in that order with Form one students sitting in the first rows for all to see the new batch that would preserve the future of Press Lake Varsity, its values and so on. The routine was simple, the girls noted:

Prayer said by someone.

Song from the mandatory hymnal.

Announcements by the teacher-in-charge and Prefects with something noteworthy to say.

On to class everyone then went. It was that simple; or seemed simple, Bridget concluded.

Bridget and her crew of friends amidst other freshmen then headed toward the freshman building. As to be expected, form one classrooms were the easiest to find and was situated far, far away from the Seniors! Hmm! Bridget thought for a moment before letting it go. What was the point? It was so centrally located that even a stranger could easily find the building that housed the fresh crop of students. Situated at the furthest end of the west campus the building stood alone – isolated as the students it served.

But it was welcoming with the surrounding huge trees separating it further away from the rest of the campus. It seemed like an island and a solemn one at that that invited students to proceed but quietly cautioned them about the perils of being too confident about anything. Just be you, the atmosphere seemed to whisper. Be you but listen as well or else.

As Bridget and her girlfriends walked along the pavement toward their classroom, they could not help but notice the lawn. It seemed so well groomed, they wondered how it was done or who did it. Nothing seemed out of place. Midway they stood to enjoy the view. It was breathtaking. Endless spans of green lawn interspersed with thriving trees, and newly painted buildings in three colours: white, hunter green and banana. Odd choice of colours that seemed to work perfectly, at least to these girls who were trying to find their bearings in a new environment. The bushes and floral patches by the administrative offices seemed well-groomed with nothing out of place. The campus atmosphere was an epitome of order – it gave an air of inflexible order. Bridget felt a sudden rush of chills. And at that moment she felt sad, then happy then unsure. Was she up to the task? Were they all up to the task? Maybe Magda and Annette who had passed in list A. For all she knew, she might become the weak link academically and socially in this newly formed group of theirs. She hoped not.

They finally arrived at the building. Good thing they were all placed in Form 1 A with 35 other strangers as Bridget would constantly refer to her other peers. As they stepped into the room she gave a huge sigh of relief. They were officially Press Lake Varsity students – college students! She giggled and chose the first seat by the door. It wasn't quite clear to her why she did this; but she just felt it would be the best place to spend the entire academic year in the first form. Her desk stood in the first row proudly. She felt proud of herself momentarily then unsure again. At that she quickly placed items on the desks next to hers and called for the others to join her. Annette took a look at her corner and walked straight across the room in search of a perfect spot. Bridget was dismayed as she watched Annette wipe off the dust from her desk and arranged the skirt of her uniform carefully on her seat. Not one time did she look in Bridget's direction. Instead, she gazed out of her window at the beautiful scenery oblivious to the immediate chaos that reigned in the classroom as students scrambled for seats.

Bridget had seen enough of that attitude and was disappointed. She turned around in search of the other three. Florence took one of the desks she had carefully reserved for her crew, and so did Sarah. But when she turned around to look for Magda, an unknown boy took the one closest to her, which she had reserved purposefully for this young friend of hers. The boy stared at her defiantly and poked his tongue out at her. She made a move to slap him then restrained herself. How dared he mess up her plan? How dared he? She looked across the room and spotted Magda who didn't seem as though she had noticed her reserving a spot for her. Like Annette, she seemed so far away. Bridget's face dropped a bit. Not what I expected at all, she chided herself. Be more forceful next time, she reminded herself. And finally she settled to her lot in the classroom. At least, she got two of her friends to sit by her. Not bad. Well, it could have been better. She was unsure again.

Did it really matter? Perhaps not. That was when she sighed aloud her frustration for all to hear. Poor timing, for the drum sounded and the Math teacher stepped into the classroom. He stopped in his tracks and looked at the class of weary students rushing to stand in his honour, to welcome him as the god of Mathematics. He frowned. They waited standing there patiently. The furrows on his forehead deepened.

"Did I hear someone sigh just now?"

No response.

He walked briskly to his table right next to the board and waited.

"Again, who is the wretch that did that?"

Dead silence but for heartbeats that drummed loudly.

"Okay," the teacher stacked his textbooks and began writing something on the board.

"Bring out pieces of papers. We are going to have a test right now," he announced without bothering to look at the students. "Remain standing!" He smiled and turned around to face the class. He heard someone at the corner fidgeting.

"Yes?" He walked toward that section of the room rubbing his palms gently with a piece of chalk in between his middle and index fingers. "Yes, little man, do you have something to say? So you are the wretch!"

Now visibly trembling, the guy that stole Bridget's seat pointed in her direction.

"Ah ha! The wretch is a girl. One of those who does not even stand a chance to pass Math." He walked closer to her desk and leaned over almost spitting in her face.

"So it is you?"

She remained silent.

"It is you who is the wretch, not so?" He barked at her.

"No sir; I mean, yes, sir," she admitted standing straight in his honour.

"Good. Now, sit down wretch; and you all!"

Bridget sat down and buried her face in the overflowing skirt of her dress. She could not bear to look at the other members of her class.

Mr. Abanda introduced himself writing out his name in full on the black board.

"Mr. Joseph Abanda; B.A Hons, University of Ibadan." Then he turned around and stared down the class before adjusting his glasses that kept sliding down his nostrils. "Not that some of you will make it that far. But what do I care. It is my job to teach young empty vessels with the hopes that they will become government stooges someday. Isn't that so, little man?"

"Yes, sir." The boy who had ratted on Bridget answered.

"Good; now back to Maths."

There was a great sigh of relief as the students opened their desks to bring out the required textbook. Mr. Abanda lectured rapidly, filling the whole board with numbers and equations. Bridget dried her tears and tried to focus on the lecture. She turned around and saw others writing frantically. Weh! Was she that dull? She thought and felt tears gathering around her eyes again as she contemplated the worst word that could better describe her predicament at that moment. The dullest girl in Form 1 A! The thought annoyed her and she said "No" several times in her head and started scribbling numbers and equations too at a feverish pace. No! Forty-five minutes flew by quickly and soon she heard Mr. Abanda announcing that as a rule he never announced his tests. He only gave impromptu tests, so they should be ready. The drum sounded off so loud the zinc creaked. Mr. Abanda dropped his chalk and gathered his material watching students scramble to their feet as he left them in peace. He was a Math god indeed as he swaggered out there adjusting his glasses but without a backward glance. Before slamming the door shut behind him he mumbled that they were all wretches anyway and some were even idiots. He laughed heartily and disappeared. His laughter continued to echo long after he was gone. Phew! The students exhaled and sat down. Bridget was at least relieved to know that she wasn't the only wretch in that class. It was the best thing she had heard in all forty-five minutes that Mr. Abanda had spent in their class. And she was content to simply be one more wretch and not the only wretch. Yes, indeed.

She opened her desk to switch textbooks in preparation for the next subject. Little man leaned over to apologize. She ignored him. Then a thought occurred to her. He was worse off than she; he was both a wretch and a little man. This new awareness consoled her a bit. She had just settled her books on her desk when Florence tiptoed over to tell her ashia. They were still chatting about the incident when Mrs. Ndonge appeared opening the door slowly and pushing her beautiful self into the room. Bridget gasped. She had never seen a woman that pretty so up close. There was excitement in the class and feet shuffled with the boys trying to contain themselves while the girls simply gazed in stupefaction. She stood there and waited for all to stand up before waltzing in like Ms. Meme.

"That is much better," she said and dropped her books on the table. The air behind her was loaded with some kind of sweet smelling perfume. Bridget sniffed the air repeatedly. It smelt good. One day, it would be she standing in front of a class and smelling sweet like that, she thought and looked away. Okay, thought disappear let me concentrate or else I may not even make it to CCAST for the advanced levels. The bubble in her head vanished and she sat upright and waited for further instructions from the goddess of English.

Leaning on the edge of her table in an impeccable lavender cotton frock that could only have been bought from Printania or Monoprix, Mrs. Ndonge laid out her class rules:

No whispering in class.

Absolutely no cheating. When she stated this rule, some of the students giggled.

She stopped and looked at them for a few minutes. The giggling stopped. She continued.

No tardiness.

She wrote these three rules on the board and asked the students to write them down in their notebooks. Then she added: these are just the first rules you should know. She smiled the whiteman kind of smile that showed no teeth and before they could figure out that it was a smile, it had disappeared and it was back to business.

"Now let's begin by testing your vocabulary power. Bring out your exercise books let's see how well they taught you how to spell in that primary schools of yours."

As the class turned to a fresh page in their books she brought out a special textbook from her stack and waited until the ruffling ceased.

"Okay; word number one." She enunciated the word stressing the different syllables as she was taught in England. Students scribbled what they thought was the right spelling.

"Good. Now the word . . ." By the time they were done she had called out ten words for them to spell out. When the last students finished spelling the last word, she asked them to exchange their exercise books and bring out their pencils.

Teacher: Circle every word that is spelt correctly.

Students performed the act.

Now, who can spell word number one for us?

She looked around for volunteers. Two hands went up.

"You over there."

First volunteer attempted.

Teacher: Wrong.

Next volunteer attempted.

Teacher: Right. Your name?

Student gave his name and teacher noted it down in her special book.

Teacher: Word number two and so on.

When they had reviewed all ten words she asked the students to return the notebooks to the rightful owners. She watched them doing this making a mental note of who was more efficient in executing her orders and who was sluggish.

Teacher: All those with ten words correct raise your hands.

None.

Teacher mumbled under her breath then looked at the class again. Bridget could see a wicked glint in her eyes and the whiteman's smile took over her lips again.

Teacher: Nine words correct, raise your hands.

One hand up.

Teacher nodded. "Pretty good, young lady. Your name?"

"Sarah."

All eyes turned in her direction. Bridget exchanged glances with Magda who had a strange look on her face. Bridget tried to figure out what it meant but could not really pin it down. Did she sense fear in Magda's eyes? Disbelief? Envy? That could not be it. Okay, it could be it. Contempt. Yes, that was it. Could that be it? It should. It was. Was not? Was? She shrugged it away and paid attention to what Mrs. Ndonge was saying next.

Teacher: Eight correct?

Three hands flew in the air.

She nodded as she counted them. "Impressive. Your names?"

"Taku."

"Benedict."

"Rosemary."

Teacher recorded their names in her special book. "Good."

Teacher: Seven and six correct?

Six hands went up.

"Good," she said simply counting the hands twice, but not making any attempt to record the names down in her book. Bridget's was one of the six hands in the air. Like the other five students she left it hanging there for a while hoping that Mrs. Ndonge would ask for their names. She could see that Magda's hand was also in the air. She beamed. Mrs. Ndonge said nothing after counting the hands.

Teacher: Those who had all ten words wrong raise your hands.

One hand up.

The teacher raised her head to see who it was. So did everyone else in the class.

Teacher: Name?

Annette.

Teacher recorded the name in a special column in her special book.

"Deplorable. Indeed, deplorable," she mumbled. As she put her pen down all eyes were still fixated on Annette. She looked away sans fou!

Unbelievable, was all Bridget could think of at that moment. Why own up to such a disastrous performance when there was no way the teacher would have ever found out? Unbelievable! She stared at the corner of the room where her girlfriend sat. Look at her sitting there and admiring the great outdoors as though all was fine with her. Unbelievable! For a moment she did not know how she felt about Annette. Or what to make of her. Then she got annoyed. Was Annette toying with them? Yes, that must be she was doing. Annoyance turned into resentment. Who did she think she was, playing with them like that-eh? Look at her sitting by the window as though all was fine. I wish I knew who her parents were. Note to self in my head, check out her parentage. Rich? Poor? Okay, who cared! Bridget smiled and pushed those idle thoughts away so she could properly focus on class work. She heard the English teacher saying something. What was that again? Think, think, listen, listen, focus, focus! Much better. Now she heard her clearly.

Teacher: If no one told you, I will be your class mistress for the academic year. Whiteman smile, normal face, serious eyes. The impeccable dress brushed aside once more as she leaned forward to pick up her books from the table. The drum sounded and the apparition disappeared just the way she had arrived leaving the door slightly ajar for the wind to toss it from side to side until someone had the good sense to shut it behind her. No one in the class had that foresight. Not even Bridget who sat so close to the door and who felt the draft each time the wind shifted its direction and pulled the door further away from its ledge or pushed it gently toward the edge. It never got it right and the door just kept going back and forth rattling as the wind brought in some kind of fragrance or odour from the natural world to the students who needed something more than education as the billboard out there by the highway proclaimed to all the parents and to the rest of the world.

"Shut that door, you Michelin," a male voice shouted from the back of the room. Bridget turned around to seek out the person. Unable to do this she shrugged her shoulders and remain seated. She wasn't Michelin. Was there a Michelin in their class? If so, she would get to meet her one of these days. Little man got up and shut the door before giving her a dirty look. Bridget remembered then that she needed to talk to Annette about the spelling exercise. Phew!

Later she would. No, now. No, during breakfast. No, later. She grinned.

Later that day when she asked Annette why she had raised her hand to let the world know of her ignorance, her friend had simply smiled.

"She wrote my name down in her special book, didn't she?"

"Yes, but."

"That was all that mattered to me. Getting my name in that bloody book of hers!" Annette gave them a white people's smile.

Bridget backed off. "You are scary."

"I know," she replied simply.

The others could not make any sense out of her response. But they nodded anyway – acknowledging their own ignorance in not understanding their friend's behaviour. It was a good place to be emotionally and they sought refuge in that space for that moment looking forward to siesta and anything else that might come after that. Admitting ignorance could be powerful. Weren't they all ignorant of something?

Bridget reflected some more on this as she slowly drifted to a well deserved sleep – that afternoon. It was all right to be stupid then? She still did not know and no one had taken the trouble to explain to her why it was not. But it felt good to be ignorant at least for that moment. It felt good to be . . . Wait a minute. Her dream was interrupted as someone claiming to be her new Big tapped her on the arm to read a letter her father had sent declaring that someone her Big with a capital B I G!! There went her ignorance right out of the window. She succumbed to her tired mind and drifted to a deep sleep that would postpone the reality of her new life at Press Lake Varsity. Well, at least for that moment.

# Chapter Six

When she got up from her deep slumber reality waited her right there by her bedside.

"Bridget?"

"Sister."

"You will have to bring your box to my dorm and place it under my bed."

"Okay, Sister."

"I mean now."

"Okay, Sister."

She got up and like a zombie in a trance took her suitcase to her new Big's dorm. Her Big's bed leaned against the wall at the farthest end of the room. It was the top bunk that had been carefully separated just like the ones all four seniors in her dorm occupied. Under this bed that was higher up than some in Dorm B she could see two suitcases stacked up high according to size on an old metal trunk. She placed hers next to these and got up to leave.

"Not yet," her Big said.

She turned around with a puzzle on her face. Her Big was smiling. Her lips twitched on the sides and her eyebrows knitted. Bridget stood on guard watching the cunning smile that surfaced and lasted longer than she would have cared. A smile so different from Mrs. Ndonge's but so equally odd! Perhaps it was a black man's smile. She watched her Big come off her bed and adjusted her wrapper around her tiny waist before dragging her two rope slippers out of there. She dragged passed the first, second and third bunk beds. At the fourth that leaned against the wooden locker wall, she stopped and beckoned to her. Bridget took small steps toward her. When she arrived her Big whispered something into her right ear. She could not understand what she was saying. The Big noticing this confusion pushed her lips in an upward direction suggesting she looked up at the owner of the top bunk. Bridget raised her head and saw the girl, who also stared back at her a little confused. Sister Catherine ignored them both and dragged herself back to the comforts of her bed. After all, it was siesta time.

"Bridget," she called softly from across the room. When the young freshman turned around Sister Catherine mouthed to her that, that was her new sister. What? Bridget was disoriented. She could not make sense of what her Big was trying to say/ Her sister? Yes? No? She felt a certain amount of revulsion in her stomach as the stub where her umbilical cord had hung began to hurt terribly. She exhaled. Okay, Bridget, she told herself in her mind; you can handle this. She looked up and caught the girl's eyes again. This time she noticed something that looked like spite; but then in a flash it disappeared and she noticed a sweet looking, rich girl now sitting upright and waiting for her to acknowledge her. She was dressed in a lovely floral nightie looking fresh and smelling fresh like the lavender flowers that dotted the fabric. Her soft cotton sheets and acrylic blanket flowed generously on the edge of the top bunk bed that suspended in the air. Store bought linens Bridget concluded curling her lips up. The girl might have noticed, for the spite returned in her eyes. No! Fire this time daring her to think any less of her. As if to flaunt her superiority as the preferred college daughter, she adjusted her matching housecoat over the nightie and sat up waiting.. Bridget had seen enough. On the girl's face was written Babylac all over – a typical spoilt rich kid! She sighed and wondered what Magda or Annette would have done. No chance of her ever finding that out now. As though she was admitting defeat she waved at the girl.

"Good," the Babylac responded and looked at their Big for further instructions.

"Go back to sleep now, Camille. You too, Bridget," their Big said from across the room. It was clear at that point that Bridget now had a family in Dorm C. As she left careful not to disturb those already enjoying their siesta she saw Sarah sleeping on Sister Dahlia's bed. The girl was sound asleep looking extremely comfortable in her nice cotton house coat – Daddy had sent that one just before school started. At the edge of the bed another one dangled. It was Sarah's *real* favourite in soft pink until Sister had decided that it was her favourite too. Bridget suppressed a chuckle. The silk robe dangled there waiting for its new owner, and Bridget figured the matching gown must be shielding Sister Dahlia's body as the Senior Prefect made her rounds to see if all was fine in the different dorms.

Agh!

Sarah's beautiful clothes! Bridget swallowed a cuss word that was forming deep in her throat. Annette laid there reading a book. She waved as Bridget left their dorm. Bridget smiled in response. Why did Annette have to see "her family troubles?" She knew her friend had seen all and heard all that had transpired between she and her Big, and she and Camille. That was not fair. Was anything fair anymore, she wondered.

Siesta that day slid away slowly leaving Bridget tired, exhausted and upset. She became even more upset when the drum reminded her to get ready for the mandatory sports. As she joined the others in her orange sports apparel, she bumped into Magda looking tall and quite fit in hers.

"How can you still look cool in that thing?" She scuffed.

"Thanks."

"Thanks for what?" Magda was really getting on her nerves.

Her friend ignored her grouchy mood and held her hand. They strolled in silence for a while.

"You know you could have ended up with Sister Dahlia," Magda reassured. They both laughed.

**47**

"You're so right." Too busy feeling sorry for herself, Bridget had not thought about that. They laughed all the way to the field, passing by Dorm C without even bothering to check on Sarah and Annette. What was the use? Then her forehead crumpled. Magda noticed.

"You, worried about Florence?" She turned around. "Oh, there is Annette."

The new girlfriend squeezed between the two of them panting hard. "Move over, Magda. I like to be in the middle."

"Since when?" Magda asked shifting on the side to create more space.

"Since now."

"Sarah?"

"Why ask me? Is she not with you?"

"No!" Magda looked dismayed. "Dorm mates my foot." She left pouting.

"Florence?"

"She is sick," Annette responded. "I thought you knew."

"Already?" Bridget sounded concerned. At that moment Sarah joined them adjusting her sports uniform that looked blatantly different from theirs.

"Wait a minute! Who sewed yours?" Annette stepped back to admire the stylish look Sarah dunned.

"Someone from home!" She beamed. "You thought I was going to wear that prisoner uniform that you all have?" She laughed hysterically. "Not me."

"So we are prisoners now?"

Annette was beginning to lose her temper. She brushed her hair vigorously and held it in a neat bun. It was already beginning to lose its lustre. Perhaps it was time for a touch up with the hot comb again.

"I did not say that."

"What did you say?'

Sarah ignored her and focused on Bridget.

"Florence is sick."

"Anyway, better that way; oya, let's join the others."

When they arrived at the hand ball court two teams were already forming. There was no time to decide who would be part of which team or not. They simply gravitated toward one or the other and the game began.

At first, it was slow and boring with team mates still warming up and trying to understand each person's game. Then it became fierce. Bridget noticed it first when Magda on the opposite team was breathing down her neck making it impossible for her to get the ball or to throw the ball to the right team mate. Phew! She finally understood that the other team was playing to win. Okay, if that was the case, she told herself then she too would play to win. The game intensified with balls flying back and forth and the goalies catching or running after hard balls that came at lightning speed. Even Annette her teammate was now covered in sweat. She would walk on the side occasionally to wipe off sweat from her face and then just like that she would leap in the air to block off shots or to steal balls. She looked fierce up in the air catching and passing the ball with such speed and skill Bridget wondered if she had not played in a team when she was in primary school. No time to think. The ball landed and she caught it and bounced it a bit before passing it along. Magda came from nowhere again and tackled her. Not this time; she dribbled and aimed the ball far away. It was unbelievable. Bridget saw Sarah on Magda's team run after the ball. She was impressed, especially since Sarah had conspicuously larger breasts than all of them. The game went on at such a fast pace with key members of the teams defending, attacking, dodging, and scoring goals upon goals. And then the drum sounded putting an end to their fun just as it put an end to their misery when they were in class. Games time was over and Bridget's team had lost barely. She cornered Annette and exchanged high fives. Then they walked to the sidelines to head back to the dorms before it was too late. She was not quite out of the field when she felt someone rushing toward her.

"We beat you people."

"Magda, why am I not surprised?"

The girlfriend still panting from the game laughed hard rolling on the grass. Noticing that no one else was joining her there she stood up.

"You are no fun!" Magda walked away dusting the bottom of her sports shorts.

That evening after dinner Florence joined them for Prep. She looked flustered.

"Wait a minute," Bridget said and was about to carry on with the conversation but stopped. Florence gave her a stern look for a few minutes before softening up. Her eyes wondered around the classroom searching. Bridget could not fathom what it was she was looking for. Then she noticed Florence smile broadly as she observed a boy in the middle row adjust his seat under his desk. He craned over and blew a kiss toward Florence and started making faces. She sighed and covered her face with both hands. Bridget had seen enough. She walked over and dragged Florence by the hair.

"You stop acting cheap right now."

Florence shoved her hand away. And sat back down.

"I thought you were ill?"

"So?" Florence pulled her sweater closer to her body and waited for Bridget to say something. When she failed to do so, Florence opened her desk and brought out a packet of butterscotch sweets. She then looked at the boy's direction and mouthed the words "thank you."

He nodded understandingly. Bridget did not get it for at that moment she had her head buried in her homework. Florence exhaled and brought out her text book to read. She was just a girl after all. A Press Lake girl? She was not sure yet. Anyway, how different could Lake girls be from Sea or Hill girls? That was something she would never know. Girls.

# Chapter Seven

Life went on as usual at Press Lake Varsity with the girlfriends adjusting at their own pace, Bridget would want to believe: Pray, Perform chores, Eat, Play, and Prep! Oh, and serve BIGS! She capitalized it in her head. But in reality she had simply come to the conclusion that there were good Bigs, better Bigs, and BAD ones with capital B A D! She thought harder and felt she was missing one other type. Oh yes, Bigs like Sarah's that were hard to place or to fully understand with their generous smiles that stretched from ear to ear and shrilled voices that stung the ears. But . . . Bridget let the thought hanging. She remembered Annette saying that every Saturday night Sister Dahlia entertained one male guest after another with Sarah watching them down her Orange drink and slowly deplete her packets of cabin biscuits and sweets. But then again, it was this same Big who would not let Sarah do any chores in the dorm or even do her own laundry. No way, Annette had heard her whisper to another senior. Sarah was too valuable she had mentioned – whatever that meant. So she made random freshmen do the chores! Urgh! The thought of it made Bridget want to throw up.

Bad Big; Good Big; bad, good Big, Bridget concluded in her mind.

Then there were Bigs like the one who OWNED Florence! Outright BAD!! She sighed and looked away. That girl had done so many dishes over the past two months it was no longer funny. Wash Sister's plate; wash Sister's friends' plates. Make Sister's bed; wash Sister's clothes and sheets; buy Sister puff puff. Braid Sister Jane's hair; her senior friends', her small friends' etc. No wonder her fingers were always sore. A thought crossed her mind and she smiled. Clever girl that Florence! I would be sick more often, if I were her. The drum sounded and Bridget sat upright and waited for the gods of subjects to walk in and teach them how to pass exams or to remind them of how stupid they were. And truly her most "favourite" god stepped in with their test papers under his armpits. Mr. Abanda! How could a man look so darn handsome and yet be so mean? She wondered as she waited for him to do something; no, say something; no, write something. Whatever. He dumped the test papers on the table and did something. Standing in front there he truly looked like a god. Then he turned to the blackboard and started scrawling equations and numbers, mumbling explanations as he went along. Bridget and the others copied notes frantically not wanting to miss a thing whether they knew what it meant or not. It just might appear in the next test; if not, in the final exam. He stopped suddenly and began pacing back and forth mumbling something.

"Oh!" They heard him exclaim and watched him scratch his forehead. He ran out of chalk and walked back to his table to get some more. Then he realized that he was yet to return their papers. He shuffled them carefully and returned them on the table before gazing at the class of forty students in neat rows.

"You wretches want your tests back?"

No Response.

He scratched his head.

"I suppose so." Snatching the tests he walked toward the window and leaned leisurely and crossed his legs. It was indeed a good position. His dead eyes gazed through them piercing a hole through the walls that separated them from the surrounding bushes or nature however one chose to call it.

"Max, the wretch," he called out.

One student dashed forward and collected his test.

"Susan, the wretch." And so on until all the test papers were gone. When Bridget got her test back she was extremely disappointed, for she had expected to perform much better this time around. It was the fourth test they had taken in Math and her best mark had remained at 10 out of 20. Now she got 9? She sighed out her frustration again before realizing what she had done. She covered her mouth and wished that moment away, but it had already caught up with her. The drama again as Mr. Abanda's cold eyes shifted to her direction. She could feel them burning a hole in her head. The pain was already excruciating. And at that moment she longed for panadol tablets. Her head throbbed.

"Who was the wretch that did that?"

All eyes turned toward her. Bridget stood up and faced the class. Her head throbbed even more. She felt as though it would burst open and her brains would spill over.

"Two hours hard manual labour," Mr. Abanda droned.

"Your name?" He asked bringing out his pen and writing pad.

"Bridget."

"Yes, indeed; you are the same wretch." He wrote down the name and tossed the pad aside.

"Sit down, wretch."

She sat down gathering the skirt of her uniform to wipe her eyes before the tears came out. The drum sounded and it was time for Mr. Abanda to leave. She heaved in a sigh of relief when he stepped out and the door closed gently behind him.

That whole week did not go so well for the girlfriends. Annette talked back at a Senior in her dorm and had to kneel by the older girl's bedside for two hours while others took siesta. Magda flunked Biology and accused the teacher of being unfair. Two hours manual labour. Sarah turned down the advances of a Senior her Big had spent weeks trying to match make them. Big mistake! She received a note the very next day asking her to return stuff she was not even aware that he had sent. He took the trouble to list them: three packets of butterscotch sweets; two packets of cabin biscuit; ten cans of sardines; one bottle of ketchup; and a bottle of grenadine syrup. Then later, he had caught her eating garri in the dining room with her fingers. Two hours hard manual labour. Urgh!

And Florence? Bridget turned around and saw a vacant desk. Hmm! That was odd. Why did no one tell her that she would not be coming to class that day? She made a mental note of it and let it go and waited for the god of French to leave and make way for the goddess of English to take over. What did it matter, anyway? They all controlled her destiny. The drum sounded and instinctively she stood up and waited for Mrs. Ndonge who waltzed in like the goddess she was. Half way close to her table Mrs. Ndonge noticed that one student was still sitting. Magda! She quietly stepped out and waited for the atmosphere to be just right before she could take over. All eyes now turned toward Magda. She still would not stand up. Sarah hurried over to see what was wrong and found her sleeping. She tapped her arm and in her confusion, Magda farted loud. The class burst into laughter.

"What?" Then she saw Mrs. Ndonge by the door. She brushed off the drool on the corner of her mouth and stood up quickly. It did not matter anyway, for the moment was perfect with everyone standing up and fearing what Mrs. Ndonge could do to them. The precious English teacher strolled in and went right to her table. Bridget concluded the girlfriends were falling apart. It was too soon, she noted then frowned. But why them and not the others? They were all falling apart. No! she disagreed with her thoughts. 'Yes,' it told her. Why? It sneered at her and whispered to her, 'you are all weak girls – not fit to be in Press Lake!' I am not a weak girl! She said to herself. But her thoughts were louder. 'You are, but you do not want to admit it.' She heard the

English teacher tell the class to sit down. Like a zombie she dropped to her seat, but her thoughts would not let her focus. 'Weak girl, she heard it say repeatedly.' No! 'Yes!' Exhausted from the struggle she caved in and started sobbing. Her sobbing sounds grew louder as her thoughts reminded her of how weak she was. Soon her head was on her desk as she convulsed into more tears making louder crying noises.

Mrs. Ndonge stopped writing on the blackboard and looked at the poor girl with a strange look in her eyes. She could not begin to fathom what had possessed her.

"Madam, she is ill; very ill," Annette offered an explanation walking toward the heap of flesh that made endless noise at the other end of the room.

The English teacher nodded understandingly.

"Take her to the sick bay."

Annette packed Bridget's books in the desk and helped her up to her feet. The tears were still pouring when they left the class to study in peace and headed out to seek appropriate help. At the sick bay, the Dispensary Prefect gave her some tablets to calm her nerves and asked Annette to take her friend to the dorm. Moments later, Bridget was sound asleep in Annette's bed snoring loud. Her friend adjusted the covers over her and watched her a little bit longer to make sure all was fine.

But Annette did not return to class for the remaining four periods. Instead with Bridget sound asleep, she changed into her "civilian" attire and headed down the road walking briskly and twirling her handbag. The dirt stretch that linked their campus to the main highway was not really that far. She was determined to get out of there and blend with the town folks for a change. She did not know why; but she needed some air far, far away from the structured life that Press Lake Varsity offered, with Bigs that were incapable of helping themselves. She sighed. How would she know that when she did not even have one? Her mind went blank

55

as she thought of her uncles and aunties who had put money together to make it possible for her to attend a school that prestigious. What would they say if she dropped out? No way. She would never do that. Her father was a simple CDC labourer but he would not let that happen. Tears swelled in her eyes at the thought of her father. She did not even know how her parents looked like anymore. It had been so long since they dumped her with her rich uncle and his wife to take care of her as their own. And they kept passing her around from one successful relative after another without bothering to ask her opinion. She laughed. Was that ever possible? She shook her head to the contrary.

Annette arrived at the main gate. The sharp metals did not intimidate her. She would not let anything come between her and her goal. And right now it was to get to the other side. Yes, she finally said it. She smiled as she climbed over the tall gate that was supposed to keep strangers out as it protected the innocent students on the campus. Out there, she felt the breeze brushed the sides of her hair, which she had carefully placed in a thick, tight bun. It felt good. Her heart raised with fear and excitement, for she knew what it meant if someone caught her in town gallivanting. She would be DISMISSED. The Senior Prefect had drilled this into their heads at orientation. She laughed out loud then turned around to return. Her heart sank. Just what if? It sank even further as she thought about the implications of what she was about to do. No! She would not let this happen to her. She was too tired of the daily structured activities in the classroom, in the dorms, in the dining room – everywhere. Besides, no one would notice. Press Lake girls are not like that! She burst out laughing. Well, this girl will be the first; at least, just this once. A thought crossed her mind. Perhaps she should buy a few sticks of Bastos cigarettes and experiment. She relished the idea so much laughing hard. She would really be a bad, bad girl! That intrigued and frightened her at the same time. Would she or would she not? Unable to resolve this she brushed the idea off her head and concentrated on her mission. Bad, bad Lake Girl, she chided herself!

She had not gone far when a black 504 Peugeot skidded to a halt next to her. She moved out of the way to make room for the car. Instead, the driver wound the window down and asked if she needed a ride. She thought a bit and accepted the offer.

"Good; enter then." The driver leaned across the passenger's seat.

"So how are you, fine girl?" The respectable older man inquired.

She smiled, "I am fine, sir."

"Good to hear that." He started whistling slowly following her as she continued to walk on. "You need a ride somewhere?"

She hesitated a moment before telling him that she wanted to get a few items from the market.

"I understand. I will drop you there in a minute."

Annette hesitated.

"It will be okay; come-on in," he insisted. Annette stood and contemplated for a brief second then shook her head against the idea.

"It's not that far off."

The middle aged man laughed. «You think I am a bad man?"

Annette ignored him.

"Come-on!"

She looked away taking a few more steps down the road. Taxi drivers honked at her. She edged close to the car with her dress brushing the door of the man's car.

"See, you'll get yourself killed. Just come in let me be a good Samaritan for today at least."

Annette's eye brightened. "In that case. Okay." She slid in the passenger's seat and they joined the traffic.

He smiled at her and adjusted his rear-view mirror. "You go to school there?"

"Yes, sir."

"Good. Fine school."

"Yes, sir."

He smiled sheepishly and made a right turn into a parking lot in front of an imposing building.

"Let's grab something from there before I drop you off, Eh?"

Annette fidgeted on her seat. "Okay, sir."

"No, no, no!" He protested. "Stop that 'sir' nonsense. Sparks, eh?"

Annette looked at him funny. She had heard of Sparks and his womanizing ways, but had not realized he lived right there in Kumba. He looked old. She made faces again and looked away.

"Well, I don't know-oh," she replied tentatively.

"Ah, you too; what don't you know, na?" He leaned forward to get a better view of her profile. He liked what he saw: young, innocent, and confused! Just splendid.

"Okay then," she said simply.

"Okay, what, fine girl?" He taunted her.

"Sparks."

"Fine. You see? Not a hard name to remember."

He opened the door to leave. "Are you coming?"

She looked at the building again. "Hotel Tranquille."

"No!" She shook her head to the contrary.

He walked over to her window. "Not hungry?"

"I'm fine."

He coughed and looked at the building again.

"Come on. Just small lunch, na?"

She smiled.

"That's my girl. You remind me of my daughter," he added laughing as he touched her arm fondly. Annette stiffened and waited for him to open the door for her. He leaned further and pushed the door gently toward her. When she came out she took in the scenery. Every inch of the area was as gorgeous as the gossip went. But then she remembered that it was a place where rich men took bad girls to. The Senior Prefect had warned them to stay away from such places. A cold chill overtook her entire body and she rushed back to the car.

"What now?" Sparks asked. His voice was unusually sharp as though he was scolding at a child.

Annette remained adamant.

He sighed and joined her in the car.

"Maybe next time, eh?" he attempted a cunning smile that reminded Annette of Bridget's Big.

Annette nodded. He did not ask her name, and she did not offer to tell him.

He smiled again and got back to the car.

"Next time, here again?"

"No."

"Playfair, then?"

She nodded.

"That's my fine girl." The cunning smile disappeared as he drove her to the market. Once they arrived he pulled to the side of the road. The smile returned.

"Here; take this and buy something nice, eh?" He squeezed a paper note into her hand and continued smiling.

"Thank you, Papa."

He frowned as he wagged his index finger, "no, no, no!"

"Sparks."

"That's more like it." His eyes wondered all over the little girl's developing figure and finally settled on her small bosom. He stared at her chest momentarily then looked at her face again. Pretty thing just about ready, he thought licking his lips. Annette arched over trying to make her budding breasts disappear. He looked away and without further ado zoomed away from the crowded street leaving a dust storm for pedestrians to sort through on their way to the market. Some began coughing hard while others simply cussed. Holding her handbag tight, Annette crossed over and found herself into the historic market. Only then did she open her hand to see what he had so generously given her. Ten thousand francs. She whistled. Never in her life had she seen a note with figures that large. She panicked and quickly hid the windfall away in her purse. A thought crossed her mind. Was Sparks one of those "bad" men Sister Dahlia had warned them about? She shook her head to the contrary. He could not be a predator. He seemed so nice and kind. And besides, he had said she reminded him of his daughter. Annette was at ease now. Her conscience was clear. She lowered her eyes to assess the development of her bosom. Well? They looked okay, or was she mistaken? A look of uncertainty clouded her face. She arched forward to hide her tiny breasts from the eyes of the world. At that moment, she felt sorry for Sarah.

Her thoughts shifted to Fese and she remembered what had really prompted her to sneak out of campus. Although she wanted to convince herself that she was doing it for Fese's sake, she knew in the depth of her heart that it was not totally true. She needed to get some air, and what better reason to fulfill this wish than her friend's crisis. So without wasting time anymore, she entered the stalls and bought snack items she felt would soothe her ailing friend: Cabin biscuits, sardines, peak milk, hollicks, and longka sweets. On second thoughts she walked the one block to Nyamsari department store and purchased a nice Made in India nightie for herself. She felt good. She had used only a quarter of Sparks' money. She still had a lot of change to spare. Enough to last her the rest of the term.

Annette was pleased with herself. She was about to hail a taxi back to school when it crossed her mind that it might be nyongo money that she was spending like that. Her eyes reddened. Just what if Sparks wanted to use her for some kind of underground ritual to appease some evil spirits?

Her face dropped. Could he be that devilish? No? She shook her head to the contrary. Perhaps not. Yes? No? Annette wrestled with this thought some more then dismissed it. She would not let the thought spoil her day. But it kept cropping up. She sighed and held tight to her purse. And just like that she brushed the thought out of her mind the same way she had let it in.

When she arrived back on campus, everyone was at lunch. Good! That meant no Prefect would suspect that she had broken any rule. She quickly sneaked out of the taxi and returned to the dorms. Moments later back in her school uniform she queued in line with a few late comers. The dining Prefect wrote down the names, but when he came to her he looked at her flustered face and smiled.

"You are late, little girl!" He reprimanded her.

She stood and waited for him to write down her name. He did not ask her name and neither did she offer. He shooed her in.

"Thanks," she said simply and hurried in. The freshmen were already serving food at the different tables. She went over to Magda's table.

"You taking food for Fese?"

"Who?" Magda seemed a little irritated as she served the others. Annette saw an extra plate next to Magda's. "Never mind," she said and crossed over to her table. Florence was still not around. She sighed and adjusted her dress before sitting down. From the corner of her eyes she could see Sarah. She also noticed how the table head eyed her friend. It made her uncomfortable. The lecher! She cursed under her breath.

Like everything else life was becoming familiar and more predictable with little surprises every now and then. And like the rest of the students they had learned to cope and had come to accept the routine as a way of life at Press Lake Varsity. She prayed that Fese should regain her strength.

# Chapter Eight

B y the time the term finally came to an end they were all exhausted from drills and activities. Bridget looked a little less chubby, her father had commented one morning when he dropped off bread for the school breakfast program. Sister Catherine had also noticed and wondered out loud as she tried to figure out what she would tell the girl's father if anything bad should happen to Bridget. Not a chance of that ever happening though. Bridget had dismissed it.

Anyway, Florence had made two more disappearing acts but had finally succumbed to the reality of life at Press Lake Varsity. As the last day of the first term drew near the girls were excited and could not wait to return home and share their experiences with their homies or to compare notes with former primary school mates now in other institutions of higher learning – the preferred term, Bridget had learned from her Big, Sister Catherine.

The campus was swamped with cars and trucks as parents, relatives and underpaid chauffeurs stopped by to haul stuff home for some students. It was not unusual to spot relatives carrying pieces of luggage on their heads to neighbouring streets. The excitement in the air was infectious with students dreaming or sharing dreams of how they would spend Christmas once they returned home. The last day of school could not come fast enough for most of the freshmen who could not wait to go home and boast to all that they were now college students. Amidst all this frenzy it sneaked up one bright day when all had almost given up hope it would ever happen. Like a typical tropical day making way for a long awaited dry season, the day broke with some clouds outshining the sun. It was a struggle but when the sun finally burst out from behind the clouds nothing could contain its heat. The rays blazed on students' head making several to itch frantically scrubbing out dandruff that had gone unnoticed or had been ignored for some time. They stood there in rows in front of the Assembly Hall in great anticipation of what awaited them in their respective classrooms. One more time their hunter green cotton uniforms almost blended with nature as students brushed by the newly trimmed hedges and stampeded on the lawns whose grass they had spent the entire term cutting. Bridget could see the Senior Prefect standing in front of the Assembly Hall directing students to the lawn. With one hand up to shade his eyes from the harsh ray of the sun he urged the class prefects to maintain order. It was hot but no one cared anymore. Soon the crowd dispersed to their respective classrooms. There was pandemonium everywhere once again with students heading in different directions searching for their class masters or mistresses. The Senior Prefect looked tired. He stood there and watched them running every which way. Bridget and her friends simply walked briskly. By the time they arrived their classroom Mrs. Ndonge was already there waiting. Today was different even for her, Bridget noticed. She was dressed but in bubba and wrapper with her headscarf carefully balanced on her plaited hair. In that attire she truly looked like a goddess of something.

As they rushed in she simply beckoned for them to sit down. No time for the usual protocol. She would smile occasionally and motioned to the new arrivals to take their seats. Even her smile was different Bridget observed. No teeth; no grin; just dimples sinking further on her cheeks as her lips curved into a smile. Was this the same woman who had taught all of them parts of speech, sentence combining, idioms and so on over the last four months? Unbelievable! Bridget pinched herself back to reality and sat down.

Mrs. Ndonge did not bother to make any speech; not that they expected any from her. How would they know? It was the first time they were receiving a report card from college. She simply handed out report card after report card without commenting on students' performance. That was odd. However, when Annette picked hers up Mrs. Ndonge stared at her for a moment and grinned. It was just one moment and one needed to have been paying close attention to even notice this brief moment of weakness. Bridget did notice. She made a mental note and waited for her turn. Report card.

Go

No comments. Hmm!

By the time the pile was gone, Mrs. Ndonge had handed out all 40 report cards. She stood up and left without the slightest indication of her being aware of the commotion right there in the classroom. Unnerved by the pleas from those who had failed and unimpressed by the celebratory notes from those who had passed, she left the students on their own.

Bridget looked sad wishing the English teacher could have at least said something. Perhaps, wished them a joyous Christmas or safe trip back home. No such luck. A sneer appeared on her lips and she dismissed the woman from her thoughts. Back to her report card.

She peeked at it first with one eye. Unbelievable! Now she had the courage to open it wide and go over the different subjects. Unbelievable, she mumbled searching for her friends to share her good fortune. She saw Sarah. The girl was beaming. Bridget smiled and left her alone to enjoy that moment. She decided to look for the others. She could see Magda jumping up and down and Florence running blindly toward her direction. The teary girl embraced her several times thanking her but Bridget did not understand why. She tore herself from the long embrace and went after Annette. The girl stood by the window looking so isolated it frightened Bridget. Her report card lay on the desk.

"Annette?" She reached out to her friend.

"Not here. Later."

"Okay." They headed for the door where Magda had relocated still jumping and kissing her report card. Bridget knew at that moment that she had to bring the girlfriends together – perhaps for Annette's sake.

"Sarah? Florence? Magda?" She called out as she searched frantically for each one of them. They were nowhere to be found. She sighed. "Annette?"

"Right here, Fese."

"Okay. The others? Let's see if we can catch up with them."

Once outside they could see the girls rushing down the pavement with the other students whom they believed had made it. Bridget exhaled.

"You deserve it," Annette congratulated her.

"Thanks. You want me to look at yours?"

"Okay." Annette took it out of her bag then she changed her mind. "Wait."

"Annette?"

"Okay." Annette handed it over resignedly. They both made the sign of the cross before Bridget took a peek at it. "Unbelievable!! Stupendous!!"

"What? Fese? That bad."

"Not at all. Unbelievable. See for yourself." Bridget offered her the report card.

Annette hesitated. "Give me." Before she could open the report card Bridget was already on her crushing her with a big bear hug.

Tears flooded Annette's eyes. "Thank you, Fese." She managed to free herself from the hug.

"Number three! Unbelievable!"

"I said that already."

"True."

Together hand-in-hand they strolled down the overcrowded pavements taking their time to admire the trimmed hedges and well kempt bushes on both sides of the sidewalk. They waved at some of their peers from a distance and watched others dragged their luggage to the neighbouring dirt road to await their transportation. The sun shone right above them in the sky ignoring the honking from impatient drivers, the rude whining from pedestrians who were not sure whether to trespass on the beautiful lawns or to walk across the dirt road to the other side. As they made a curve at a corner to take the direct sidewalk that led to the girls' dorms Annette looked at her friend.

"Fese, any ideas on the two that beat me?"

Bridget laughed.

"Hard to tell." She laughed again. "Most likely some stupid boys."

"That figures."

At that moment little man zoomed past them then retraced his steps.

"Wretch, I beat you all." He disappeared as he had appeared holding his report card high for all to see that he had indeed placed first in all form one. Annette and Bridget burst out laughing as they watched him disappear among a green sea of students in another part of the campus.

They arrived at the dorms just in time to see Magda hop onto a Toyota bus. She noticed them and squeezed out right away. "Driver, ah beg wait small." The man honked impatiently. She ignored him and stepped down anyway to hug her friends. Then back on the bus and Abakwa Express drove off spewing smoke behind. They could hear students heading to Bamenda already chanting as their bus drove away at a frenzied speed. Bridget waved until they could see the bus no more.

"What next?"

"Sarah." They saw her by the Victoria bus. Her Big was explaining something to the driver. Sarah waved. They waved back and joined her.

"Where are the others?" She asked.

"Magda just left."

"Florence?"

Bridget and Annette exchanged glances.

"Perhaps her dad picked her up already."

"Perhaps so, Sarah." Bridget glanced at her watch. "I don't know when my father will be done over there."

They looked across the street and saw her father's car packed by the kitchen.

"I have to wait for him before heading home."

"Annette?"

She looked away. The conversation ended. Sarah hopped on the bus and bade them bye. They watched the bus slowly pull out of the curb and picked up speed. As it drifted further with one of their girlfriends just like Magda's they waved harder as though to freeze that moment. Buea bus, Lobe bus, Mamfe bus – the buses all left but Annette did not board any.

"You want to go gather your stuff?"

"Sure, why not."

As they slowly walked to the dorm they saw Florence running toward the road excitedly. They turned around to see a new car pulling by the curb. Florence ran blindly toward the car and waited for the driver to turn off the engine. Annette's face creased.

"Papa, Papa," Florence screamed. Her father came out of the car with opened arms. He embraced his little girl.

"Flo, how are you, my little darling?"

"Fine, Papa." Then she remembered. "My report card."

He let her go and opened it. "Excellent! Come hug your dear old Papa, na?"

She rushed into his arms one more time and he engulfed her. Annette and Bridget watched the daughter-father spectacle dumbfounded. Then Annette noticed the car. She took in a deep breath and tried to escape but Florence was calling them to come greet her Papa.

"Papa, my friends," she introduced them. He shook their hands and concentrated on his daughter.

"Where is your luggage?"

"Over there, Papa." She pointed to her dorm where she had carefully arranged her travelling bag and suitcase.

"Let's go get it then, eh?" He started walking toward the luggage but Bridget stopped him.

"We can take care of that, Papa."

He obliged them and the three girls brought Florence's stuff to the car. Her father arranged them in his boot.

"There! All fitted so well with room to spare." He dusted his hands and looked at his daughter once more.

"Your friends need a ride somewhere?"

Florence turned to them. "Eh?"

"Not really," Bridget responded. She was touched by this kind gesture.

"Good then." Mr. Ewang opened the car and took the driver's seat once more.

"Florence, greet your friends and hop in." She did as she was told. When she had settled down in the passenger seat her father looked at her.

"Hungry?"

Florence laughed. "Of course, Papa."

He smiled back.

"You think your friends may be hungry too?"

She pushed her head out of the window and shouted. "You people hungry?"

Bridget was not sure how to respond. "Annette, what do you think?"

"I'm not in a hurry."

Bridget glanced at her watch one more time and looked at her father's truck across the street. She was not certain when he would be done with the bursar.

"Why not?"

"Good," Mr. Ewang said. "Hop in both of you then."

He drove off.

"Charcoal Grill?"

"Yes, Papa."

He smiled. He knew his daughter liked the stockfish meal prepared in that restaurant. He was hoping that her friends would be as thrilled with the experience as much as his Flo.

The meal was great as always but the three girls stuck to themselves. He liked their camaraderie. So he left them there for a while to go check on something. When he arrived hours later they were done eating and were waiting.

"Thank you, Papa," Bridget said.

Florence laughed while Annette grinned.

"Don't mention it, my daughter. Hop in let me drop you off."

At that he drove them back to the campus but as he was about to branch out of the highway a thought crossed his mind. He adjusted his rear-view mirror.

"How about some meat pies for later?"

Without waiting for a response he headed toward an old resort and grinded to a halt next to the entrance. The girls' eyes lit up as they mouthed the name "Monte Carlo" to each other. They had heard a lot about the place but could not begin to fathom that it was so old and so secluded. The surrounding trees hid the property so well. Annette felt uneasy. In her mind she wondered if it was another place where rich men took bad girls to. At this thought, she arched her back again to hide her chest. The others did not notice this impulse.

"Out, you all."

The girls got out and followed him in. They saw him talk to the manager who nodded and wrote something down.

"They do not have any ready at the moment. Anyway, I promised you all meat pies and I am going to give you meat pies."

Florence started to protest that it would take too much time and her friends might miss their ride. He stopped her midway.

"Okay, Papa."

He ordered some pineapple juice for them and they sipped it slowly while waiting. Half an hour later the manager appeared with a plateful of meat pies.

"Can you wrap them in foil paper for us to go?"

The man nodded and did just that.

Mr. Ewang paid and they left the building. He lagged behind waiting for the girls to go ahead. As they walked by him he held out a hand to Annette. She looked apprehensive momentarily and then decided to take the hand. They walked in silence and when they got closer to the car he slipped a note into her hand. She took it and crumpled in a ball then dashed forward to the car. She already knew what it was. He smiled at her. She hurried over to Bridget's corner. He understood.

The car ride back to the campus was uneventful. Florence and Bridget chatted all the way there sharing ideas on how they would each spend Christmas while Annette listened. When he dropped them off and was about to leave he put his head out and smiled at the girls.

"Florence, all that talk about Xmas got me thinking."

His daughter grinned not getting his point.

"Here, Bridget; something for Xmas. And you too, Annette." He gave them a thousand francs each.

Bridget was taken aback. She hesitated for a moment but did not want to come across as ungrateful, so she took it.

"Thank you, Papa."

"Thank you, Mr. Ewang," Annette said.

"No problem." He drove off with them waving at Florence who seemed equally as impressed as they both were.

"What a kind man!" Bridget said unfolding the one thousand francs note.

"I bet, he is," Annette mumbled.

# Chapter Nine

Three weeks went by fast and before the girls knew it was back to school for another term. Florence and Magda now looked somewhat sophisticated with stretched hair painstakingly clipped into a ponytail with hair bands and pins. Magda accentuated hers with bobby pins that had little white bows. They were surprised to see Bridget and Sarah's still looking plain with their neat afros. Granted this was the look Press Lake Varsity encouraged, but they could not understand why their friends stuck with it even while on holidays. As plain as Sarah could ever looked. Annette was another case. No one had seen her at all the entire week. But that first Saturday of the term a different car dropped her off. The girlfriends saw Annette edged out of this old, battered cream Renault 4 straightening her dress. She then leaned over and took something from the driver who was covered with dust. They could hear the man reminding her to manage. She nodded and stepped out of the car's way. The car groaned away spewing toxic fumes in the air. It sounded like an animal in pain as it made its way out of there. Annette waited until it disappeared before carrying her stuff toward the dorm. Her friends dashed out to meet her halfway.

"Give me that." Bridget seized a fertilizer bag from her hand.

"What happened?"

Annette handed over the envelope.

"What is this?"

"School fees."

Magda sighed. "Was that all that kept you behind?"

"Leave her alone," Sarah barked.

Surprised at the sharp tone, Magda turned to her friend. "What's your own there?"

"Just leave her alone." Sarah repeated looking away. She knew it was just a matter of time before she too would start missing weeks of classes. Unless her father sent the money on time, her mother had said.

Florence ignored them. "Anyway, we are glad you came back."

Annette looked at her funny. "Why was I not going to come back?"

"Well, you said . . . "

"Florence!" Bridget hushed her.

"Okay."

They escorted her to her dorm and watched her unpack. On her vono bed all five sat down pushing the springs to the floor. Magda noticed.

"Bridget, you take the metal bucket."

They burst out laughing as she turned it upside down to convert it into a stool.

Annette unpacked slowly taking out one beautiful new dress after another. A pair of jeans, a maxi dress, a flare skirt, a new blouse . . .

"Your Xmas must have been something." Bridget jumped up from her makeshift stool and seized the maxi dress. It was long and gorgeous. Bridget placed it against her figure. "Nice!"

"What are you talking about? Just look at the new pair of shoes!" Florence was tickled. She tried them on and found out they were slightly larger for her size 37 feet. "They are beautiful. I bet you cannot wait till the next social!"

They all giggled watching Annette put the last clothing item away. Then to the fertilizer bag. The moment she untied it they knew they were all in for a treat. Annette enjoyed that moment taking her time to unwrap the aluminium foil that had the cake her aunty-in-law had baked for her. Then the chin chin and fried fowl. Finally, she brought out the egusi pudding and meondo that were at the bottom of the stash. Now the real smiles.

"My sister, you did it-oh!" Bridget complimented.

"I knew you people would be expecting it."

They heard the drum sound for dinner. Magda sighed. "That's not for us tonight."

The others concurred as they gathered around the bed and feasted on the goodies. All weekend they avoided the dining hall with its predictable menu of beans and weevils as they dined on leftovers from home supplementing their diet occasionally with puff puff they bought down the road.

And so the second term progressed for these girls who had come to school to study in order to become major players in their communities some day. At the very least, to become loyal civil servants with no aspirations other than to live *really well!* Anyway, only Bridget ever thought about that these days. Everyone else was busy thinking about something else. May be about life in general and what it had in store for them as they motivated themselves every morning to go to class and deal with one god of something after another or to return to the dorms and deal with one semi-goddess or wanna be semi-goddess.

Hard as Bridget tried to make the group work she could still notice as the weeks unfolded that something was not quite right. She was losing control of her girls – her girls! Yes, so she had begun to refer to them in her head. They were hers and no one was going to change that. This feeling of something not being quite right started to eat her up as she watched her friends closely from a distance and from up-close. Then one evening as they headed to class for Prep she remarked to Annette that there was something amiss.

"Florence, you think?"

"No," she whispered to her friend. "I can feel it deep inside me. It is Sarah!" She said in a cocksure manner. They both stole glances at the other three not far behind them.

"Is she bigger?" Annette gestured with her hands.

"Ah, you too. No. Florence, may be, but that is not the point."

Annette was puzzled by this.

"It does not bother you that Florence spends most of her weekends stretching her hair these days?"

Florence hurried over. "You said something?"

"No!" they replied in unison. Florence dropped back and walked gently behind her friends.

Bridget coughed. Annette turned sideways to listen more.

"Sarah. Watch her tonight," she said turning around to address the others at the same time. "Hey, people, hurry up before we are late."

"Are you people done with your gossiping?" Magda laughed.

Annette stopped in her tracks, "I don't gossip. You of all people should know that by now."

"Okay, I was just joking."

"Right!" Florence and Sarah exchanged glances.

"Why do you people do that?"

"Bridget and Annette exchanged glances."

"Okay, I meant it, hang me if you can."

The drum sounded and they hurried into their classroom for Prep. No sooner had they settled down than for a form two boy to walk up to the Senior that was supervising that week and whispered something into his ears. He nodded and the boy eyed at Sarah. She got the message. Moments later after the boy had departed from the class, Bridget saw Sarah pack her stuff and left. The veins in her neck stuck out as Bridget curbed her disappointment. All night she watched the door for Sarah to return in vain. She coughed to draw Annette's attention. Her friend winked at her in understanding, got up and requested permission to go to the bathroom.

Out there she searched in vain. Sarah was nowhere to be seen. Annette returned to the classroom and took her seat. Bridget looked at her direction and she gestured that she could find her nowhere. Bridget requested permission to take a bathroom break. Sure, the Prep supervisor said but only for ten minutes. She left and searched as well. Sarah had to be somewhere around the academic buildings, she postulated making sure her eyes shifted from window to window, and at times behind shrubs. She walked along the sidewalk scrutinizing the different couples making out. When she finally saw one girl she thought was Sarah, she tugged her away from the boy's embrace. The boy cursed and reached out for the girl. Bridget ignored them and was about to check out the next couple when she heard someone warn them about the "guyless chick" spying on people. Embarrassed, she ran back to the classroom and concentrated on her homework. The drum sounded and behold Sarah appeared from nowhere. Her face looked as impeccable as it had been when she had gone out, with all her make-up in place. No creases on her dress either. Bridget wondered what was going on. Annette told her it was none of her business. That was how little they knew of her, Bridget reminded herself. They were all her business whether they liked it or not. They became her business the day they had all agreed to her rules. Yes, they were her rules and they had all agreed to abide by them. Her eyes became teary.

That night and every other night thereafter one freshman after the other came to seek permission on Sarah's behalf. Each time one of the girlfriends would go out to spy but always to no avail, for they could never locate her once she stepped out into the dark night to meet with someone. Bridget got fed up and decided to confront Sarah. Sarah reminded her that it wasn't her "bloody business!" Big mistake. Bridget vowed never to talk to the "harlot" again. Sarah said, "fine." And the rest of the crew but for Annette remained clueless as to what had actually transpired between those two.

"Nothing," Bridget said.

"Nothing," Sarah said.

'Okay," Magda concluded. "Be that way!" Neither Florence nor Annette bothered themselves. They simply let their friends not talk to each other. Then one day Sarah told her Bridget was too old fashioned. Annette kept her mouth shut and began scrutinizing Sarah's every move in their dorm. Night after night in her vono bed she would observe from the corner of her eyes as Sister Dahlia discreetly brought in one male prefect after another and then laughed her way out of there for half an hour or so to check on something in another dorm. It became Sarah's duty to entertain these older teenage boys, happyly listening to their stories and smiling loudly. They were after all seniors. Annette did not know what to make of it all. She was almost certain everyone in the room was equally as surprised as she was and if not perhaps disgusted with both Sarah and the seniors who came visiting at ungodly hours every weekend. She snuggled under her covers and strained her ears to catch fragments of Sarah's conversation with the seniors. It was difficult but she could hear her laughing hard. This forced her to sit up and pretend to search for something. The laughter turned into more giggles. Annette was embarrassed for her friend. Her face darkened as she noticed the others watching that corner of the room intently as well. It was a spectacle she no longer wanted to see. "Bad girl!" she mumbled dragging her cover over her head to obliterate the show.

The next day, she told Magda. Magda wasted no time to tell Sarah off. She said Sarah was a bad girl with capital letters: BAD. Sarah ignored and sought her way into the classroom. Magda pinned her against the classroom wall and warned her to change her behaviour before she disgraced all of them.

"Leave me alone!" Sarah screamed.

"That's all you have to say?" She yelled back not caring who was listening.

"You leave me alone now, Magda. Am I your relative?"

Magda was infuriated by this blatant dismissal of their friendship.

"But you are a girlfriend!" She replied relaxing her grip as she endeavoured to control herself. Ignoring the crowd that was already forming in front of their class, she carried on, "You must promise us now."

Sarah gave her a dirty look and wrestled her way out.

"You are not my mother!" She brushed the chipped paint that had crumbled all over her blouse collar from the wall.

Magda charged after her. "Promise?"

"Promise what, you Fox?"

Magda heard Sister Dahlia. She smiled and let Sarah go. "Nothing, Sister; nothing."

"I thought so," she turned to Sarah. "Go wait for me in the dorm."

"Okay, Sister." As Sarah left, Sister Dahlia took another look at Magda.

"You Fox like this; you need to be taught a lesson."

Magda looked around for a sympathetic face but there was none there at that moment. She waited for Sister Dahlia to finish.

"You so, tonight at my bedside at nine, you hear?"

Magda nodded rubbing her hand as she sensed doom in the air. When she had the courage to look at the faces again, her eyes met with several. It was incredible. Each one of those eyes harboured fear. Unbelievable as her friend Bridget would say. The thought brought a smile onto her lips and her courage was restored – just like that.

"Excuse me," she pushed through the crowd looking for a way through to the classroom. She was almost out of there when she heard a familiar voice. It came from not too far from where she was heading. She pushed harder and almost bumped into her three other friends.

"What is going on?" Bridget asked.

"Never mind. It is now over." She winked at Annette. "Let's get out of here."

Florence led the way to her dorm, a place she deemed safer from the inquisitive eyes of the dorms B and C rowdy crowd. But when they arrived she noticed that her Big and her friends had taken over her bed. Bridget, Magda, and Annette watched from a distance. Florence sighed and turned around to face her friends. "It is like this every day. Sometimes, I wish I was on the top bunk like the other form one girls in my dorm." She stood there and waited for someone to come up with a solution.

"Our dorm, Magda?" Bridget rose to the occasion.

"Why not?"

As they headed out Bridget whispered something to Annette. Magda sighed.

"Why do you two whisper all the time like we are not around?"

"Okay," Bridget admitted defeat. "You see what I mean about Sarah not being like before?"

Magda's face lit up. "All the whispering was about Sarah?" They looked at her.

She laughed again. "Who does not know the kind of girl she is? Don't bother whispering. We all know! The entire student body knows!" She threw her hands up in frustration.

"No!" Annette said. "I will not condone this."

"Oh?" All three friends asked. They were all confused. Florence drew closer.

"She is what her Big wants her to be; I see things night after night and that is that."

"Care to share the details?"

"No!"

"No need to shout at us then," Bridget reminded her. "We get your point. You see things; we see things; everyone sees things. And it is always about Sarah!"

"Stop it!" She ran off and left them alone.

The weeks passed and they forgot about the incident as always and went on with their lives. Then the tests started coming one after the other like war. The girls did their best. Well, all four of them since, they no longer knew anything about Sarah. They had collectively decided it was better to no longer discuss her affairs. Rather, they would wait for the phase to pass or for something bad to happen to her. But nothing did! Day after day, Sarah passed them by the corridor without acknowledging anyone. She also ignored them in the communal bathroom each morning and evening when they took their showers together. Instead of suffering from her behaviour, she was looking radiant and smiling all the time with lots of freshmen hanging around her wanting to braid her hair or to do something for her. How could this be? Bridget wondered daily as she searched for signs of remorse from their dear friend. There was always none forthcoming. Bridget concluded that she had failed Sarah woefully as a friend and it was time to let her friend be whatever she desired for herself.

As she nursed her wounds one day in class oblivious to what was going on, she heard Mr. Abanda, the god of Math laugh. That got her attention and she sat upright to listen to what he had in store for them.

"My, my, what do we have here? A love letter!" Mr. Abanda looked up from the book.

"I didn't know you wretches could write love letters. How amusing." He paused.

"What do you think? Should I read it or not?"

No response.

"Okay. Your opinion does not count and will never count for anything anyway." He paced up and down the room and brought out the sheet of paper from the exercise book.

"My Sweet heart,

*The first time my eyes landed on your succulent body, I knew you were the chosen one. Every night when I think of you, my heart goes pata pata, pata pata!"*

Mr. Abanda paused. The corners of his lips twitched. He turned to face the board and laughed. When he faced the class again he had a stone face.

"Who is the wretch who wrote this nonsense?"

No response. Some students began to giggle.

"You find it funny? Eh, Wretches?"

No response.

He began pacing back and forth examining individual student's faces. He stopped by Bridget's desk. "Are you the one who wrote this?" Before Bridget could respond he brushed her away with a head shake. "Not capable of romance." Bridget was embarrassed. She recoiled further into her seat and resisted the urge to sigh. He walked away and continued reading:

*The other day when I saw you carrying a pot of beans to the refectory my heart pounded so hard I thought it would burst open. I watched you rationing beans to those nine ungrateful bastards at your table and thought 'I wish I was in form five; no one would make my girl soil her delicate hands in dirty palm oil.' At that moment I longed to touch those lovely hands of yours once more, remembering the last time they had caressed my chest after I had cleared your grass.*

*Sweet heart, always remember that your catarrh would always be my butter; your sweat, my mimbo; and your beautiful limes, my pillow. You are . . ."*

"Enough of this rubbish!" Mr. Abanda closed the book he had found the letter in. Bridget looked around the room to see if the owner was there. Then she noticed Florence's hands under the desk trembling. She looked away.

"What is wrong with you wretches?" He looked at the name on the back of the book.

"Florence Ewang, the wretch of wretches! Come take your wretched book before it contaminates my hand."

Sarah burst out laughing as she noticed Bridget recoiled further in her chair.

"Ewang, the wretch?" Mr. Abanda called out again.

No response.

"Okay then." He dropped the book on the side of his table and noted on the list he sometimes used to conduct roll call, "absent!" He spelt it out loud for all to hear. It was at that moment that Sarah stood up to claim the book.

"I am she."

"I bet you are. Why am I not surprised?" Mr. Abanda scratched off the absent he had written down next to Florence's name. "Come get your book, Ewang the wretch," he said holding the book for Sarah at the same time letting his eyes feast on her developed body.

"Pig," Bridget said under her breath.

After class Sarah handed over the book to Florence.

"Thank you," she said.

"For what?" Not waiting for her to respond, she added, "doesn't it feel good to know that there are things that others will never know about you?" Sarah had that wicked glee on her eyes that dared Florence to disagree. Florence did not know what to make of this.

"I am nothing like you!"

"Uh-huh, so you say."

The boy who had written the letter to Florence stopped by to comfort her but she brushed him off.

"Leave me alone." He was taken aback.

"I just wanted to . . ."

She would not let him complete the sentence.

"Do I know you? Go away, you Unclean!" He flustered. She slammed her desk shut and stormed out of the room. But not fast enough.

"The lover, I suppose," Sarah laughed over her shoulder. "What a joke!

"You shut up there!" Florence disappeared not noticing the sadness that had replaced the sneer on Sarah's face.

# Chapter Ten

And so the second term unfolded revealing sides of the girls they knew nothing about as it brought out hidden strengths they were unaware they each had. Florence dumped her "boyfriend" for a week then reconciled with him after he sent a few of his friends to come plead on his behalf. She dumped him again when he ate too much dodo and threw up in the refectory, and was later branded "Dodo Head." She told her friends that she was through with him. A week later he sent her a card expressing his love for her. He would die if she said "no" to him one more time. In the envelope he included a drawing of a heart with an arrow shooting through the heart. Then a scrawling to compliment the image: "Pomme de mon Coeur." How romantic. She shed some tears and told her girlfriends she was really through with him. But that weekend Bridget spotted her leaning against a wall next to Dodo Head. He was begging her to let him kiss her and she was fighting off the urge to succumb to his wishes.

"Disgusting!"

Florence froze.

"What now?" He turned around and saw Bridget. "What is with you, this guyless chick?"

Florence ran away. "I didn't mean it that way," he apologized running after her.

"How did you mean it, Dodo Head?" Bridget sneered. "You want her, you will have to pass through me."

"Look at you a mountain of flesh," he said and left.

Bridget spat on the ground. "Disgusting pig!" She did not know what Florence saw in the guy. "Even if na jam pass die, she would never stoop that low," she mumbled in

Pidgin English. With no one close by to notice, she raised her arm and checked her body mass, then sighed. "Bush Pig!" She was not that fat. She was simply healthy and only matured boys were capable of recognizing that. She walked back to the dorm passing couples making out in the halls, behind trees, on benches etc. They were everywhere. How disgusting. The nocturnal activities were revolting to her. She decided to pretend not to notice what was happening around until she was finally out of the academic buildings. Only then did she heave in a sigh of relief. Moments later, she was in Dorm A searching for Florence. She was nowhere to be found. Her bed looked unkempt as though she had not made it all day. Then Bridget remembered that it was the meeting spot for form five girls in that dorm— seniors who could easily crush the likes of little Florence. How sad.

Sarah! Ah, that one too was still carrying on with her form five boyfriend. The thought disgusted Bridget. But why? She searched for reasons in her head in vain. Perhaps she was jealous. Was she? No way! Yes? No! She dismissed the thought. How could she be jealous? She was only thirteen. If she had wanted to, she would have secured a boyfriend as well. She thought about it and realized that third term was half-way gone and no boy had approached her. Was it that bad? Not really, she consoled herself. Then nodded in agreement: Bad, bad, bad. She was Michelin, wasn't that what Dodo Head was implying? Was that the reason why no one had ever shown an interest in her? Her mother said she was pretty; her girlfriends thought she was pretty. She looked at herself in her mind's eye and saw a beautiful face staring back at her. That was not the issue then. They were simply afraid of her. Those immature boys in her class; who needed them! Get out of my head, Fools; she snapped the useless thoughts away.

A new week began with its own challenges. This time it was Magda. The other girlfriend with no "better half" as Bridget had begun describing them – the guyless chicks.

Like Annette too. What was wrong with her too? Nothing, Bridget concluded. That just proved her point. They were tough. That was what she thought until she entered class and saw Magda's head buried inside her desk and she was reading a note. She waited for her friend to share the content of the note later on as they headed for the dorms, but she said she had already destroyed it. Here: she offered them butterscotch sweets. Annette whistled. "Someone has a secret admirer."

"I guess so. It came with the note. Isn't that sweet?"

Annette peeled her sweet and started sucking it. "Tastes good and expensive."

"I don't care," Magda dismissed it. "It was on my desk when I came to class."

Bridget said nothing.

Another note was taped to Magda's chair when she went to class the next day. It simply said "Would you be my lover?" She crumpled it and tossed it out of the window. Big joke! During Prep there was a package on her desk. Her heart began to pound as she opened it in search of a note. No note. She shrugged her shoulders and opened the gifts anyway: biscuits and more butterscotch. Whoever was interested in her must be loaded. She shrugged it away again and shared the stuff with her friends.

"You got a note again?"

"Yes," she responded casually. "Something about becoming his lover – whatever that meant!"

"I bet Sarah would know," Florence added. All eyes turned toward her. "Just a thought."

Sarah ignored them.

"If he was man enough, he would talk to me in person and not hide behind notes and gifts."

"But don't you find it romantic?" Florence was unsure whether she was saying the right thing or not. She searched her friends' eyes for assurance, but there was none forthcoming. She sighed. How she missed her boyfriend!

"Biscuit, anyone?"

"Why not?" The four girls ate the biscuits and sweets and forgot about the secret admirer.

That is until Magda received another note a few days later. It simply said: "Be my lover!"

She tossed it out of the window but ate the coffee cake that came with it. That evening at Prep another was taped onto her chair with the same message. She tossed it out again before searching the faces in the classroom for any clues. Nothing seemed abnormal on the faces. She shrugged her shoulders and went on with her business as though all was fine. Then one evening at Prep time she came in and there was no note. She sighed and took her seat. But when she raised her head, there was a message for her on the black board for all to see: "Be my LOVER Magdalene or ELSE!" Bridget rose to erase it.

"Let it be."

It remained there until at the end of Prep. Magda then stood up graciously and wiped it off. The boys snickered; but she did not care. Calmly, she walked out of the room. Nobody would unnerve her, she decided. But the very next night there was another note on the board:

"Chop Money! Press Lake Varsity Girls, chop money!" Magda had had it. She asked for permission from the Prep supervisor to address the class. He accepted. She stood there in front of everyone and dared the boy who was doing this to step forward and face her like a man. No response.

"I thought so." Before she could return to her seat Annette was already up and wiping the board. Annette looked tensed.

"You should have left it there."

"No!"

Magda looked across the room for some encouragement from Bridget. Her friend looked equally helpless. She looked in Sarah's direction but her seat was vacant. Magda sighed.

The girl must be smooching somewhere, she concluded. "What a bad luck friend!" she cursed under her breath. Then she thought of Florence. Perhaps Dodo Head could help them identify the culprit. Florence brightened up. It was the opportunity she needed. That weekend she met with Dodo Head and let him kiss her forehead and touched some parts of her body she was not sure he should touch. He was so elated that he promised looking into the matter. But the week went by without him uncovering anything new. Florence gave up trying and told the girls that Dodo Head had tried his best.

"Did he even try?" Bridget was disgusted once more with Florence as she stood next to them chewing her Hollywood gum, which she was certain Dodo Head had given Florence as a make-up present.

"Yes, he did."

"That was it!"

Magda told her Big who drew the male Senior Prefect's attention to the problem and all hell broke loose in Form one A one evening.

It all happened so fast; Sarah could not begin to fathom how it got to that point. She pleaded with her eyes for Bridget or any of her girlfriends to fill in the blanks, but they gave her the stare. So like a classmate she had to witness the drama unfold first hand in class. Magda had walked in and headed directly to her desk. Moments later a crew of Form Five students stormed in. Feet rustled as the students began to panic. The Senior Prefect took a piece of red chalk and wrote on the board: 'Chop Money, Be my lover' and then drew an image of Lucifer next to these words. Bridget fidgeted at her seat eager to see what would happen.

The Senior Prefect wiped the red dust off his fingers and faced the class.

"Now, I want to know the truth!"

No response. The room was so quiet one could hear a pin drop.

"Who has been sending notes to Magdalene Anye?"

No response.

"I am waiting!"

He turned to the Punishment Prefect. "Jonas, what is the verdict?"

The Punishment Prefect laughed in a devilish manner: "Three strokes and one hour manual labour!"

Students gasped in the class.

"Good. You have all heard the verdict. Do you want to confess now or all suffer the consequence?"

No response.

"Okay. All girls step out on the corridor."

Feet scurried out.

"Now boys, who is it that has wet dreams they cannot control?"

No response.

"No one is willing to confess?"

He nodded. "I am proud of you I must say, for not wanting to snitch on one of your own."

The boys exchanged glances. Then Little man raised his hand. "We do not know who is doing this?"

"You don't? Eh?"

Dodo Head concurred.

"Well, at least you tried. Now line out here." The three prefects standing out there brought out their belts. Moments later the girls heard the boys shrieking in pain. When it was over the Senior Prefect asked them to quickly dry their tears and to stop squirming before they lost points with the girls. They acted accordingly, for they understood what it meant, especially those who had girlfriends in the class like Dodo Head.

"No one disrespects a Press Lake Varsity Girl and gets away with it, you hear?" The Senior Prefect reminded them. "Get that in your thick skulls." He adjusted his belt and stood upright to face the boys one more time.

"Bring the girls in now."

The Prep supervisor asked one of the students to alert the girls. As they marched in the Senior Prefect looked at them with contempt. His lips curled up with so much disdain that Bridget wondered what they had done wrong.

"You girls," he began when they had all settled down.

"If your Papa or brother didn't buy it, don't eat it! If you don't like him, don't' chop his money. If you do, it will come back to bite you!" He started to leave then changed his mind. His lips curled up again in a sneer.

"Look at you all. You disgust me! Girls, if you want to be loose, change schools. Not at Press Lake! Not when I am in charge! Never!" He sighed. Now he was done. They left the room without a backward glance.

Versions of the incident spread like wild fire across campus. One that bothered Magda the most was the version that said the SP had to protect a "Loose Form one girl from a collector." She had not done anything wrong, had she? Depending on the girlfriend she spoke with the answer was either yes or an emphatic "No!" She was confused. Her Big beat her up in the dorm for hiding stuff like that from her. "You could have been taken advantage of!" She chided her over and over again. Fat chance, Magda said in her head. Within a week of this incident she was branded a whore and a tough chick at the same time! Form four and form five boys started asking her out for dates on the nights they had socials on campus, whereas the foxes stayed far away from her. She was hot in demand but she kept saying "No" to each potential boyfriend. She was not ready. Others would promise her more butterscotch or cabin biscuits but Magda had learned her lessons. No freebies anymore! Then just as they had flocked around her asking her out for dance dates, the boys left her alone. She was a "Kaso," and no one wanted to waste his time cracking a hard nut. Magda was dismayed.

"Wasn't that what you wanted?"

"Yes. No!" She turned to her friend, "Bridget, honestly, I do not know anymore."

Bridget was shocked. "I know where I stand on these issues. You better make up your mind; either you want them to keep asking you out or not."

"It is not that easy," she began.

"Yes, it is; just take one look at Sarah. See how old she's already looking?"

"I don't want to be like her!"

"Then decide. Which do you prefer: a cheap girl or a Kaso?"

She thought for a moment then shook her head.

"Is there another option?"

Bridget thought hard and shook her head to the contrary. "Not that I am aware of, sorry."

Magda sighed. The social expectations of being a new teen weighed heavily on her. She wished things were that simple. Not! Bridget kept reminding her. Was she that weak that she was unable to take a stance? She shook the thought away. She was not a weak girl. Her father had reminded her of her strength so many times, he would be disappointed in her, if she allowed boys to manipulate her feelings.

Second term came to an end a month later with Bridget, Annette and Magda maintaining their academic ranks. Florence, the three girlfriends did not know. She refused to share any information about her results with them this time around. So Bridget concluded that she might have failed.

"I don't think so," Annette disagreed.

"Me too," Magda concurred.

"Why are you two so certain?"

They turned around and the answer was right in front of them. Sarah was crying all by herself sitting on one of her imported suitcases. She looked like a frightened kid listening to Sister Dahlia scolding her about her performance.

"Over there is a girl who might have truly failed," Annette remarked. She pitied Sarah. "What do you people say? Should we go over?" She turned to the group and noticed a wicked glee on Magda's face.

"Serves her right."

"Fese?" Annette was puzzled at the look on Bridget's face as well. It was a sneer as none she had ever noticed on her best friend's face.

"You all are bad!" She walked away without them even noticing. When they snapped out of their reverie she was by Sarah comforting her. Florence joined her there and gave the big breasted girl a hug.

"Should we join them?"

"In a moment, Magda; all in good time."

"I hear you; it's about time she wised up."

Bridget looked up.

"How can you say a thing like that when she is in so much pain?"

Magda sighed. "Trust me; better now than when we are in form five."

When they walked over to lend their support Annette was already in a taxi heading somewhere. They assumed she was heading home. In her heart, Bridget hoped the girl's relatives would fill their collection box in time for next term's fees. Poor Annette with so many rich relatives but stuck with a father whose children had to beg to go to school. She could hear the frantic horn of Abakwa express.

"Time to leave."

"I know," Bridget replied.

She saw her father's truck packed next to the Principal's office and sighed. She would wait until he was done. As she traced her steps back to the corridor where her luggage sat waiting, she saw Florence.

"You too?"

"Papa will be coming soon."

She nodded in understanding.

"Was it a good term for you?"

"Yes," Florence smiled. "I beat Bob!" It felt good to say that.

Bridget looked at her. "Is that his English name?"

"Yes."

"Good for you. I presume you did better than last term."

"Yes."

"Me too."

They both sighed and waited for their Papas to stop by soon. It would be anytime from now. They were in good company and were in no rush to leave that corridor. Not just yet.

# Chapter Eleven

The holidays were too short this time around. Too long for some like Annette who could not wait to return to a more suitable environment where she could control her space and not being bossed around by one rich cousin or aunty or uncle after another. She could live with the Bigs and their sometimes unreasonable demands – not that she had one. But she had survived Press Lake thus far only with her girlfriends.

For girlfriend, Florence returning so soon after Easter was abominable! It was doubly worse because she had to watch her favourite cousins hop on buses and returned to colleges so far away from hers. It depressed her but her father insisted that she must return to school on the first day. She wasn't ready. When would it all end? This pick up and go and when one was about to settle down to a comfortable routine it was pick up your stuff and return home for mid-term break, holidays and rubbish was becoming tiresome. She was tired and wished she were older so she would have a choice of leaving or doing what she really wanted. Life would be so perfect when that time came. In a few more years, she consoled herself.

Girlfriends Bridget, Magda and Sarah had nothing to complain about. The holidays were over and it was time to return and that was it. There was nothing to be sentimental about.

That first night back Florence spent with Bob behind the Assembly Hall, hugging and making out. He had missed her terribly he whispered nonsense verses in her eager ears. She held tight to his embrace enjoying every single moment of it. Then he tried to kiss her on the lips, she withdrew.

"What now?"

"I'm not ready for that."

"But you know it is what all lovers do?"

She twisted her face. "Are we lovers? I thought we were simply boyfriend and girlfriend."

"What is the difference, my little pet?"

He got her there and she wriggled in his arms as he tickled her. He pulled her face closer to his and attempted to kiss her again. She shoved him off.

"Okay, I will wait. But let's embrace now?"

She smiled and cuddled in his arms her back leaning against his chest. She was enjoying every moment of the experience when she noticed Sarah at another corner making out seriously. Without thinking she detangled herself from the embrace she had relished so much and walked over. Sarah was pinned against the wall with her blouse unbuttoned. This guy was all over her rubbing his face on her bosom. Florence was disgusted.

"Shame on you, Sarah," she shouted.

Sarah laughed sheepishly and began to button her blouse.

"No," the guy said gnawing on the sections of her bosom still exposed.

"Sarah?"

"Okay, okay." She shoved him away from her body.

"Why do you let him do that to you?"

"What?"

The form five student with whom she was making out pulled her back into his arms.

"Go away little girl; shoo," he brushed Florence away.

She stood there hands akimbo and waited for Sarah to come to her senses. She didn't care whether he was a senior student or not and could punish her to two hours manual labour. She wanted his hands off Sarah. He unbuttoned her blouse; Sarah buttoned it back giggling.

"Sarah?"

"Get lost, Fox. I will punish you."

"Sarah?"

"Okay." She buttoned the last open slot. "Spearman, next time."

Spearman looked disappointed. "Because of this small girl, sweetie?"

She ignored him and followed Florence's lead.

"You know I'll not be able to sleep well tonight, not so?" Spearman shouted after her.

"I know," she chuckled. Florence gave her another funny look.

"How can you be so calm? Anything could have happened."

"But nothing happened; thanks to you."

"I am not joking, Sarah."

"And your own there is what, Florence?"

Florence had had it. "Bridget was right about you. Now I understand why."

Sarah let it sink for a moment. She cleared her throat.

"You know something? I will not repeat form one as you all must now think." She sighed. "True, second term result was bad," she added.

They walked on in silent. "Florence, I don't want your pity."

"Who is pitying you?"

"You all, I know." Sarah sighed.

They had just crossed the last stretch of the corridor that linked the academic building to the refectory when Florence spotted her father's car. She let go of Sarah's hand.

"Just a second."

She made a run for it but stopped in her tracks. Sarah walked over.

"Just as I suspected; Papa is not here for you."

Florence looked crestfallen. How could that be? But it was true. He could see him chatting with someone. That someone entered his car and they drove away. Florence ran after the car as Sarah watched on.

"How could he just leave like that without checking on me?"

"May be he did?"

"Why do you say that, Sarah when we just saw him leave with someone."

"Where have you been yourself all evening?"

"True."

They separated as they headed to their different dorms. Florence had a horrible night as she pondered what her father had been doing there.

The next morning though things were back to normal and last night seemed like a bad dream. The French teacher gave them a dictation test; the biology teacher gave them a lab test; the Religious Studies teacher gave them verses from the Old Testament to memorize and life was truly back to normal for these girlfriends.

It was weeks in the third term that Bridget and Sarah began talking again. Thank God, Bridget confided in Annette. She did not feel comfortable not talking to a friend. Annette laughed at her foolishness and assured her that she was certain Sarah felt the same way too. One thing stood between them and Sarah though: Spearman! All four girlfriends were in agreement in their sentiments about this form five student whom they believed was taking advantage of their friend. He was too old for Sarah, Magda said. No, Bridget disagreed. He was too mature for their friend. Florence agreed and added that he was too sexy for her. All found something they did not like about Spearman but for Annette. When Bridget asked her opinion about the situation, she shrugged her shoulders and said that perhaps he liked Sarah. Bridget and the rest were appalled at this sentiment. But he was too old, too mature, too sexy. Annette agreed. All that and more. Case close.

Two months later into the term when Spearman warned them about the impending rites of passage tradition she wondered if they had judged him harshly. Bridget disagreed.

"But he's the one who hinted Sarah that our tails would be cut soon? Doesn't that make him okay?"

"I suppose so," she said. "Not really. Okay let me think about this some more."

"Bridget, we should come up with strategies to deal with this cutting tail business."

"Magda, you worry too much. If it were that bad, we would have heard about it a lot more." She dismissed it.

The rumours intensified about the impending "cutting tail" rite of passage. Bridget began noticing something odd. Her form two big friends had started avoiding her. That was odd. Magda, Annette and Florence confirmed her worst fears. Something was not quite right. Perhaps the "cutting tail" ritual would be worse off than she had anticipated. They searched for Sarah for confirmation but she said she knew nothing else about the procedure but was preparing for the worst like they all should be. What did that mean? Bridget had pressed on. She said she had no idea; she was just preparing – just in case.

A week later, Bridget and her friends understood what it meant. They were just settling in their dorms one evening when the lights went out without the usual warning signals. An eerie feeling lingered in the dark room. Bridget began feeling her way to her bed, but did not make it far before several unknown girls surrounded her. She could feel their warm breaths as they closed on to her. Then someone hit her on the arm. She felt a fist blow on her face. She moaned in pain trying to grope her way out of there in vain. Another blow and another but this time they were not as hard. They were pillow slugs. Nonetheless, she tried to protect herself but her arms simply fluttered in the air helplessly unable to latch onto anything or anybody to protect her from the assault. She yelled for help repeatedly in vain. She could hear others yelling as well. The fist blows intensified and one slammed her on her buttocks knocking her flat onto a vono bed. She still could not identify her assailants in the dark but their weapons varied. She tried to run out of the room but a group of students blocked the door. She wrestled with them but they overpowered her and dealt her more blows calling her the most stubborn Fox in form one. How could she be when there was Magda. She could hear her friend screaming on the other side of the room as they beat her up too. There were cries of pain throughout the buildings. She could not tell who was doing the beatings and who was doing the crying. She simply knew they were under attack.

Bridget fought hard kicking left and right. She hit one on the leg. The assailant cursed.

"Boh, over here," the person called for reinforcements. "This Fox is trying to show me something."

Before Bridget could protest a fist blow knocked her over again and pillow punches followed thereafter as they slugged her nonstop once more. A whistle sounded from somewhere and feet scurried away with their owners cussing and slamming doors in succession. All was calm in the dorms again but for the faint sobs from the students who had been formally initiated into boarding school life. The lights flashed on some minutes later. At first, the bright lights blinded Bridget. But when her eyes got used to the now much cherished brightness she looked around. The room was in disarray but older students seemed to be sound asleep. She could hear a few chuckling under their covers as some form one students continued to groan in pain.

"What are you looking at?" The dorm captain caught her eye.

"Nothing, Sister."

"Good. Go back to sleep before I punish you."

Unbelievable. She limped over to her bed. Unbelievable!

At breakfast the following morning the Dining Hall Prefect asked the servers to go collect breakfast items for their different tables. As the students got up to leave the student body burst out laughing.

"Walk upright, Servers; enough with your sluggishness" the Dining Hall Prefect commanded.

Bridget was thankful that it wasn't her day to serve. Her body was sore all over and she could see the same phenomenon among her peers as they dragged their unwilling bodies up to fetch the pots of food. She sighed.

Not a word was spoken about last night's event. It seemed like a conspiracy. She looked around and no one seemed to care. Life went on as normal. Unbelievable.

As they walked to class for their lessons, she inquired about the others' health.

They were all sore and did not care to talk about it. Then she noticed Sarah walking ahead without a care. Bridget's eyes darkened.

"Sarah, how come you are not limping?"

"I hid under my Big's bed."

"But why didn't you tell us to do the same?"

"I did. Strategy!"

"Oh! But you should have tried harder to make us listen."

She stopped. "Listen to me. Make you the almighty Bridget to listen to me." She walked on. "I don't think so."

"Okay, I get your point."

"Good."

The academic year ended exactly three weeks later. The girlfriends had all made it through form one and looked forward to the next academic year. As they exchanged addresses before breaking up for the long holidays Bridget watched Spearman haul Sarah's beautiful pieces of luggage onto the Victoria bus. His eyes seemed moist. Unbelievable! Could he actually be in love with her? Wonders would never end! At that moment she envied Sarah looking so delicate and radiant in a free flowing cotton frock her "daddy" had sent recently. She envied her just a little, she finally admitted. Spearman shook her hand and leaned forward to embrace her the way he did in the alley when no one was watching, but pulled back in time. Too many people were watching.

He blew her a kiss. She looked away a little embarrassed. She was not that experienced and wanted the world to know that. He understood and smiled. She smiled back revealing her beautiful set of even white teeth. The bus sped away sending smoke in his direction. He covered his mouth and watched her disappear. Only then did he glance at the address in his hand before placing it in his pocket. Bridget could tell he was broken hearted as she continued to watch the couple part company for the long holidays. She knew he would check her out that holiday. Unbelievable! She snapped out of her obsession in time to see Magda's bus zoom off. And there were three of them once more.

"What now?" She asked the remaining two.

"Father comes in an hour," Florence said simply.

They both looked at Annette. She was fidgeting with some change in her pocket. "I will catch a taxi later." She hesitated. "Like before."

"Good. I'm in no rush. K-Town is my town."

"Same here."

"Rendez vous Silver Club this weekend?"

"Will be there," she sat up. "Here comes Papa." Florence dashed off to the road to meet her father. Mr. Ewang pulled over and hugged his daughter as always. Her friends walked over to greet him. He shook their hands and turned his attention back to his daughter.

"Time for a quick bite before I take you home to your mother?"

"Of course, Papa. My friends too?"

"Why not?" He held the car door open for them to get in. Bridget got in and pushed further to make room for Annette. She took the seat directly behind the driver. He got in and adjusted the mirror so he could see her clearly. When she looked up he winked at her. She smiled shyly and looked away. Mr. Ewang took his daughter and her girlfriends to town and gave them the time of their lives –

one more time. It was becoming a dangerous habit. But what did it matter at that moment as they sat down in Lido hotel eating porcupine pepper soup and downing bottles of harmless coca cola? It was just a befitting way to say good bye to their freshman year and all that went with it – childhood and all; as they braced themselves for the future they wished they could foretell. Their laughter echoed down the street into the heart of Kumba town alerting every parent of the dangers that lurked around waiting for their children – daughters in particular. Mr. Ewang too, he suddenly realized as he watched the girlfriends enjoy themselves that fateful afternoon on his account. The proud papa of a teenage daughter with beautiful teenage girlfriends.